U0088105

YADAN YADAN YADAN YADAN YADAN YADAN YADAN YADAN
DAN YADAN YADAN YADAN YADAN YADAN YADAN YADAN
N YADAN YADAN YADAN YADAN YADAN YADAN YADAN
YADAN YADAN YADAN YADAN YADAN YADAN YADAN YAD
YADAN YADAN YADAN YADAN YADAN YADAN YADAN YADAN
ADAN YADAN YADAN YADAN YADAN YADAN YADAN YADAN
AN YADAN YADAN YADAN YADAN YADAN YADAN YADAN
N YADAN YADAN YADAN YADAN YADAN YADAN YADAN YA
YADAN YADAN YADAN YADAN YADAN YADAN YADAN YADA
YADAN YADAN YADAN YADAN YADAN YADAN YADAN YADAN
DAN YADAN YADAN YADAN YADAN YADAN YADAN YADAN
N YADAN YADAN YADAN YADAN YADAN YADAN YADAN YA

ESSENTIAL WORDS FOR EVERYDAY USE

英文單字只要會這些就夠

目錄

Table of Contents

人體

Body

頭部：

head (n.) 頭

詞彙：

headache 頭痛

片語：

nod one's head 點頭，表示同意

shake one's head 搖頭，表示不同意

scratch one's head 抓頭、搔頭，表示正在煩惱或思考

turn one's head 轉頭

例句：

'Are you pregnant?' She shaked her head.

「妳懷孕了嗎？」她搖頭否認。

Peter scratched his head thoughtfully.

Peter抓著頭沈思。

Mary turned her head and looked at me.

Mary轉頭注視著我。

brain (n.) 腦

詞彙：

brain tumor 腦瘤

例句：

The human brain is divided into two halves.

人腦分成對稱的兩半(左腦和右腦)。

Emotional responses are a function of the right hemisphere of the brain.

右腦主導我們的情緒反應。

face (n.) 臉、表情

詞彙：

a long face

不高興的表情、拉長(板起面孔)的臉

MP3 002

somebody's face lights up/brightens

某人的臉亮了起來，開始感到開心、快樂

例句：

There is a big smile on his face.

他的臉上綻放出燦爛的微笑。

What's the long face for?

有什麼不開心的事嗎？

David's face lit up when I mentioned Susan's name.

當我提到Susan的時候，David臉亮了起來。

hair (n.) 頭髮

例句：

You need to brush your hair before going out.

出門前你得梳頭。

I'm going to get/have my hair cut.

我要去剪頭髮。

forehead (n.) 額頭

詞彙：

a high forehead 高額頭

例句：

Iris wrinkled her forehead in concentration.

Iris專注時會皺眉頭。

ear (n.) 耳朵

例句：

Kevin whispered his secret in my ear.

Kevin在我耳邊低聲訴說他的祕密。

eyebrow (n.) 眉毛

詞彙：

eyebrow pencil 眉筆

bushy eyebrows 濃眉、粗眉

片語：

MP3 003

raise somebody's eyebrows 挑眉，表示驚訝或不同意

例句：

This decision caused a few raised eyebrows.

這個決定讓一些人大吃一驚。

eyelash (n.) 睫毛

詞彙：

long eyelashes 長睫毛

eye (n.) 眼睛

詞彙：

an eye for an eye 以牙還牙，以眼還眼

片語：

open/close eyes 睜眼／閉眼

例句：

There were tears in my eyes when I listened to your story.

當我在聽你的故事時，我的眼中充滿淚水。

Close your eyes and count to ten.

閉上眼睛數到十。

nose (n.) 鼻子

詞彙：

a runny nose 流鼻水

片語：

blow one's nose 擤鼻涕

I've got a runny nose.

我流鼻水了。

Her nose is bleeding.

她正在流鼻血。

nostril (n.) 鼻孔

例句：

MP3 004

The smell of gunpowder filled my nostrils.

火藥味(煙硝味)充斥著我的鼻孔。

mouth (n.) 嘴巴

片語：

open one's mouth 張嘴、有時候也引申為說話

shut your mouth 閉嘴！(不禮貌)

例句：

Barbara didn't open her mouth once during the meeting.

Barbara整場會議不發一語。

lip (n.) 嘴唇

例句：

He licked his lips.

他舔了舔嘴唇。

tooth (n.) 牙齒 (teeth複數)

front/back teeth 前排／後排牙齒

false teeth 假牙

a loose/missing/broken tooth

一顆鬆了／掉了／斷了的牙齒

例句：

It is very important to brush your teeth thoroughly at least twice a day.

一天至少兩次徹底清潔牙齒很重要。

tongue (n.) 舌頭、語言

詞彙：

mother/native tongue 母語

foreign tongue 外語

例句：

MP3 005

I burned my tongue on the hot coffee last night.

我昨晚喝咖啡時燙到我的舌頭。

Jack felt more comfortable talking in his mother tongue.

Jack說母語時比較自在。

cheek (n.) 臉頰

例句：

The tears ran down her cheeks.

淚水滑落她的雙頰。

jaw (n.) 下巴

詞彙：

a firm jaw 堅毅的下巴

例句：

He suffered a broken jaw in the accident.

他在那場意外中傷了他的下巴。

Eric punched Ethan on/in his jaw.

Eric對著Ethan的下巴揍了一拳。

neck (n.) 頸部、脖子、領子

詞彙：

V-necked V領的

例句：

The champion had the medal placed round his neck.

這位冠軍選手脖子上掛著獎牌。

He wore a brown V-necked sweater.

他穿一件棕色的V領毛衣。

throat (n.) 喉嚨、咽喉

詞彙：

sore throat 喉嚨痛

MP3 006

例句：

Have we got any medicine for a sore throat?

我們有什麼藥可以醫治喉嚨痛嗎？

There is a fishbone stuck in my throat.

有根魚刺卡在我的喉嚨。

temple (n.) 太陽穴

Adam's apple (n.) 喉結

手：

arm (n.) 手臂

詞彙：

left/right arm 左／右手臂

upper arm 上臂

a broken arm 手臂骨折、斷手

例句：

John has a broken arm.

John斷了一隻手。

Mary put her arms around my shoulders and gave me a hug.

Mary環著我的肩膀並且給我一個擁抱。

Joseph showed up with his new girlfriend on his arm.

Joseph挽著他的新女友連袂現身。

MP3 007

biceps (n.) 二頭肌

例句：

He has a dragon tattoo on one of his biceps.

他的一隻上臂上有個龍形刺青(tattoo)。

elbow (n.) 手肘

例句：

She sat with elbows on the table.

她將手肘放在桌上坐著。

forearm (n.) 前臂

例句：

Jason has a scar on his forearm.

Jason的前臂上有個疤(scar)。

wrist (n.) 手腕

詞彙：

wristwatch 腕錶

例句：

I sprained my wrist playing badminton.

我在打羽球時扭到了我的手腕。

He looked at the gold watch on his wrist.

他看了看戴在手腕上的金錶。

fist (n.) 拳頭

例句：

He held the money tightly in his fist.

他將錢緊緊攢在手心。

He banged the table with his fist.

他砰地用拳頭搥打桌子。

palm (n.) 手掌

片語：

read one's palm 看手相

MP3 008

例句：

John looked at the coins in his palm.

John看著掌心裡的幾枚硬幣。

After hearing Sophie's report, her boss slapped his palm on the desk.

聽完Sophie的報告後，她的老闆拍了桌子一下。

finger (n.) 手指

片語：

keep your fingers crossed 祝福、祈福

例句：

We're all keeping our fingers crossed that it will not rain today.

我們交叉手指，祈求今天別下雨。

thumb (n.) 大拇指

詞彙：

thumbs up/thumbs down 表示贊同／否定

例句：

The baby is sucking its thumb.

這個嬰孩正在吸吮他的大拇指。

They've given his plan the thumbs down.

他們否定了他的提案。

forefinger/index finger (n.) 食指

例句：

She lifted the note carefully between her thumb and forefinger.

她小心翼翼地拿起那張鈔票。

middle finger (n.) 中指

ring finger (n.) 無名指

little finger (n.) 小指

MP3 009

腳：

leg (n.) 腿

例句：

The boy is trying to balance on one leg.

男孩試著用單腳取得平衡。

She sat down and crossed her legs.

她翹腳坐。

thigh (n.) 大腿

knee (n.) 膝蓋

例句：

Charlie sat in the corner, hugging his knees.

Charlie在角落抱膝而坐。

My baby sister was crawling around on her hands and knees.

我的小妹正在四處爬行。

shin (n.) 脚脛

例句：

Betty's got a nasty bruise on her shin.

Betty的腳脛上有個嚴重(nasty)的瘀傷(bruise)。

foot (n.) 腳掌 (feet複數)

詞彙：

athlete's foot 香港腳

on foot 走路

片語：

on my feet 站著

例句：

We wiped our feet on the mat.

我們在腳踏墊上清理我們的腳。

The bus didn't come, so we set off on foot.

公車沒來，所以我們走路上路。

ankle (n.) 腳踝

例句：

Richard fell over and twisted his ankle.

Richard摔倒了，並且扭傷了他的腳踝。

heel (n.) 腳跟

詞彙：

Achilles' heel 弱點、致命傷

例句：

I've got a sore heel.

我的腳跟好痠。

toe (n.) 腳趾

片語：

on someone's toes 踮腳

from head to toe/foot 從頭到腳、全身

例句：

The little boy stood on his toes to look out of the window.

那個小男孩踮腳看向窗外。

She was shaking from head to toe.

她全身都在顫抖。

arch (n.) 足弓

詞彙：

fallen arches/flat feet 扁平足

high arches 高足弓

MP3 011

軀幹：

shoulder (n.) 肩膀

詞彙：

look/glance over your shoulder

緊張地朝後方張望

片語：

shrug someone's shoulders

聳肩，表示「不知道」（注意此處為複數）

例句：

He tapped the taxi driver on the shoulder.

他拍拍計程車駕駛的肩膀。

Jack is about six feet tall with broad shoulders.

Jack大約六呎高，並且擁有一對寬闊的肩膀。

When the teacher asked who broke the window, every student shrugged their shoulders.

當老師詢問是誰打破窗戶時，每個學生都聳聳肩表示不知情。

chest (n.) 胸膛

詞彙：

chest pains/infection 胸痛／胸腔感染

例句：

Jason folded his arms across his chest.

Jason雙手抱胸。

breast (n.) 乳房

詞彙：

breast implant

乳房矯正(一般是指隆胸)

breast cancer 乳癌

例句：

MP3 012

When a woman becomes pregnant, her breasts tend to grow larger.

當一個女人懷孕時，她的乳房會增大。

stomach (n.) 腹部、胃部

詞彙：

butterflies in the stomach

緊張導致的胃部翻攪不適，

就像蝴蝶在胃裡飛一樣

stomachache 胃痛

stomach cramps 胃抽筋、胃痙攣

stomach upset 反胃、腸胃不適

stomach ulcer 胃潰瘍

例句：

I always have butterflies in my stomach before a test.

考試前我總是因為緊張而覺得胃不舒服。

He was punched in the stomach.

他的腹部挨了一拳。

liver (n.) 肝臟

詞彙：

cod liver oil 魚肝油

belly (n.) 腹部、胃(較不正式)

例句：

The doctor asked him to lie on his belly.

醫生囑咐他趴著。

waist (n.) 腰

例句：

Peter put his arm round Carmen's waist.

Peter攬Carmen的腰。

MP3 013

The skirt was too big around the waist.

這件裙子的腰部部分太鬆了。

hip (n.) 臀部、髖部

例句：

She waited impatiently, standing with her hands on her hips.

她等得很不耐煩，兩手叉腰地站著。

The skirt is a bit tight across the hips.

這裙子在髖部附近有點緊。

臟器：

organ (n.) 器官

詞彙：

organ transplant 器官移植

organ donor 器官捐贈者

例句：

The heart is one of the body's vital organs.

心臟是人體的重要器官之一。

heart (n.) 心臟

詞彙：

heart attack 心臟病發

例句：

His grandfather died of a heart attack.

他的祖父死於心臟病發。

MP3 014

I can hear her heart beating fast with fright.

我可以聽到她因為恐懼而加快的心跳聲。

lung (n.) 肺

詞彙：

lung cancer 肺癌

例句：

Smoking can cause lung cancer.

吸菸會導致肺癌。

kidney (n.) 腎臟

詞彙：

kidney failure 腎衰竭

vein (n.) 靜脈、血管

詞彙：

deep vein thrombosis 深層靜脈血栓

例句：

Alice felt the blood racing through her veins when Tom held her hand.

當Tom牽著她的手的時候，Alice覺得熱血沸騰。

artery (n.) 動脈

詞彙：

coronary artery 冠狀動脈

例句：

Smoking is one of the causes of coronary arteries disease.

吸菸是造成冠狀動脈疾病的其中一個原因。

MP3 015

疾病／症狀：

allergy (n.) 過敏

詞彙：

an allergy to food/a food allergy 食物過敏

例句：

Jason has an allergy to cow's milk.

Jason對牛奶過敏

形容詞：

allergic (adj.) 過敏的

例句：

I am allergic to aspirin.

我對阿斯匹靈過敏。

anemia (n.) 貧血

(英式英語：anaemia)

例句：

Tiredness and pallor are the main symptoms of anemia.

疲倦和臉色蒼白(pallor)是貧血的主要症狀。

asthma (n.) 氣喘

詞彙：

an asthma sufferer 氣喘患者

an asthma attack 氣喘發作

cancer (n.) 癌症

詞彙：

lung/breast/stomach cancer

肺癌／乳癌／胃癌

例句：

Smoking can cause lung cancer.

吸菸可導致肺癌。

chicken pox (n.) 水痘

cold (n.) 感冒

片語：

have/get/catch a cold 感染感冒

例句：

Don't go to work if you have a heavy/bad cold.

重感冒時就別去上班。

flu (n.) 流行性感冒

詞彙：

bird flu/avian flu 禽流感

swine flu 豬流感

片語：

have/get/catch a flu 感染流感

例句：

Victor is in bed with flu.

Victor因為流感而臥病在床。

dizzy (adj.) 頭暈的

例句：

Mark felt dizzy and had to sit down.

Mark因為頭暈所以必須坐下。

faint/light-headed (adj.)
頭重腳輕、頭暈眼花

例句：

I felt faint with hunger.

我餓到頭暈眼花。

Iris had had several pints of beer and was starting to feel light-headed.

Iris幾杯啤酒下肚後就開始頭暈眼花。

MP3 017

fever/temperature (n.) 發燒

片語：

have a fever/temperature 發燒

例句：

Oliver was sent home from school because he had a fever.

Oliver因為發燒被從學校送回家裡。

附註：

take one's temperature 量體溫

cough (v./n.) 咳嗽

例句：

The smoke made me cough.

這些煙讓我咳嗽。

I've got a bad cough.

我咳得很厲害。

lose voice 失聲、沒有辦法說話

例句：

Zoe has got a severe cold and lost her voice.

Zoe的感冒很嚴重以致於她沒辦法說話。

hypertension/high blood pressure (n.) 高血壓

例句：

I have high blood pressure.

我有高血壓

附註：

take one's blood pressure 量血壓

heart disease (n.) 心臟病

例句：

Heart disease is the leading cause of death in many Western countries.

心臟病是許多西方國家的首要死因。

附註：

heart attack (n.) 心臟病發

diabetes (n.) 糖尿病

例句：

The universal symbol for diabetes is a blue circle.

糖尿病全球識別標誌是一個藍色的圓圈。

lump (n.) 腫塊

例句：

She found a lump in her breast.

她在乳房中找到一個腫塊。

tumor (n.) 腫瘤（英式拼音tumour）

詞彙：

a brain tumor 腦瘤

例句：

They found a tumour in his brain.

他們在他的腦裡找到一個腫瘤。

lose appetite 沒有食慾、吃不下、食欲不振

例句：

I've felt so sick and lost my appetite.

我覺得很不舒服而且沒有食慾。

indigestion (n.) 消化不良

例句：

You'll give yourself indigestion if you eat so quickly.

你吃這麼快會導致消化不良。

MP3 019

diarrhea (n.) 腹瀉、拉肚子

(英式拼法為diarrhoea)

例句：

Thousands of refugees around the borders are suffering diarrhea outbreak.

邊境附近數以千計的難民正飽受腹瀉流行之苦。

sickness (n.) 噁心、嘔吐

詞彙：

diarrhea and sickness 上吐下瀉

例句：

Drinking unclean water can cause diarrhea and sickness.

飲用不乾淨的水會導致上吐下瀉。

Some women experience morning sickness during the first three months of pregnancy.

有些婦女在懷孕的頭三個月中會有晨吐的現象。

vomit (v.) 嘔吐

例句：

Lisa was vomiting blood.

Lisa吐血了。

constipated (adj.) 便祕的

名詞：

constipation (n.) 便祕

例句：

If you ate more fiber, you wouldn't get constipated.

如果你多攝取一點纖維就不會便祕。

My wife suffers from constipation.

我老婆深受便祕所苦。

depression (n.) 憂鬱症

例句：

MP3 020

Some students show signs of anxiety and depression at exam time.

有些學生在考試期間會出現焦慮和抑鬱的症狀。

toothache (n.) 牙痛

例句：

Paul's got a really bad toothache.

Paul牙痛很嚴重。

nasal congestion/stuffy nose/blocked nose (n.) 鼻塞

earache (n.) 耳朵痛

food poisoning (n.) 食物中毒

外傷：

itch (v.) 發癢

例句：

My nose itched yesterday.

我鼻子昨天發癢。

I don't wear wool because it makes me itch.

我不穿羊毛製品因為它會讓我發癢。

形容詞：

itchy (adj.) 令人發癢的

例句：

The dust made me feel itchy all over.

灰塵讓我全身發癢。

swell (v.) 腫大

例句：

MP3 021

It is easy to tell that she had broken her toe because it immediately started to swell.

她顯然弄斷了腳趾頭，因為患部馬上就腫了起來。

形容詞：

swollen (adj.) 腫大的

詞彙：

a swollen hand/knee/foot

腫大的手／膝蓋／腳掌

cramp (n.) 抽筋

例句：

Several runners needed treatment for cramps during the marathon race.

馬拉松競賽中，有些選手因為抽筋而必須接受治療。

rash (n.) 疹子

詞彙：

a rash on my chest 胸膛上的疹子

例句：

I have got an itchy rash all over my chest.

我的整個胸膛長滿了令人發癢的的疹子。

cut (v./n.) 割傷

例句：

I've cut my hand with that knife.

我用那把刀切到手。

Ann suffered a deep cut to her scalp.

Ann深受頭皮上一道很深的割傷之苦。

bruise (v./n.) 瘀傷

例句：

She had a few cuts and bruises but nothing serious.

她有幾處割傷和瘀傷，但情況並不嚴重。

I bruised my knee quite badly when I fell off a ladder.

我從梯子上摔下來然後膝蓋瘀青了。

dislocate (v.) 脫臼

例句：

Nicole dislocated her knee when she fell off/ was thrown from her bicycle.

當Nicole從她的腳踏車上跌下來時，她的膝蓋脫臼了。

形容詞：

dislocated (adj.) 脫臼的

詞彙：

a dislocated shoulder 脫臼的肩膀

twist/sprain (v./n.) 扭傷

例句：

Jeremy Lin is out for two weeks with a knee sprain.

林書豪(NBA知名華裔球員)將因膝蓋扭傷而缺賽兩個禮拜。

Bill slipped on the ice and twisted his left wrist.

Bill在冰上滑倒並且扭傷了他的左手腕。

break/fracture (v.) 骨折

例句：

She broke two of her ribs when she was thrown from her horse.

當她從馬上摔下來時，她摔斷了兩根肋骨。

He fractured his hip in the accident.

這場意外弄斷了他的髖骨。

名詞：

fracture (n.) 骨折

例句：

MP3 023

He suffered multiple fractures in a car accident.

一場車禍造成他多處骨折。

形容詞：

broken (adj.) 骨折的

例句：

David had several broken ribs and a suspected broken leg.

David斷了幾根肋骨。其中一隻腳也有可能骨折。

burn (v./n.) 燒傷

例句：

David was badly burned in the blaze.

David在火災中受到嚴重灼傷。

sunburn (v./n.) 曬傷

例句：

Sunscreen is a cream or lotion which protects our skin from sunburn.

防曬乳是一種能保護我們的皮膚免於曬傷的乳液。

We were all sunburned from a day on the beach.

我們都因為在海灘上待了一天而曬傷。

MP3 024

醫院：

hospital (n.) 醫院

例句：

I spent a week in hospital for food poisoning.

我因為食物中毒住院一個星期。

Victims were immediately rushed to a hospital.

受害者立即被送往醫院。

clinic (n.) 診所、專科門診

詞彙：

dental/family planning clinic

牙科／家庭計畫(生育)專科診所／門診

例句：

It is a rural health clinic with ten to fifteen beds.

那是一個偏遠的診所，提供10到15個病床。

ambulance (n.) 救護車

例句：

Please call an ambulance.

請叫一輛救護車。

stretcher (n.) 擔架

例句：

Jo was carried off the track on a stretcher.

Jo直接在跑道上被擔架抬走。

wheelchair (n.) 輪椅

詞彙：

special parking for wheelchair users

輪椅使用者的專屬停車位

例句：

She will be in a wheelchair for the rest of her life.

她的下半生將在輪椅上度過。

MP3 025

doctor (n.) 醫生

片語：

go to/see a doctor 看醫生

例句：

Have you seen a doctor yet?

你去看醫生了嗎？

surgeon (n.) 外科醫生

例句：

A surgeon removed her brain tumor.

外科醫師移除了她腦內的腫瘤。

psychiatrist (n.) 心理醫生

例句：

A psychiatrist is a doctor who treats mental illness.

心理醫生是治療心理疾病的醫生。

dentist (n.) 牙醫

例句：

You should have your teeth checked by a dentist at least twice a year.

一年至少該給牙醫檢查牙齒兩次。

nurse (n.) 護士

例句：

We'll get the nurse to put a bandage on your wrist.

我們會請護士替你的手腕包紮。

The school nurse sent Betty home.

校護決定要讓Betty回家。

blood test (n.) 驗血

MP3 026

diagnose (v.) 診斷

例句：

A psychiatrist diagnosed Vivian as severely depressed.

心理醫師診斷Vivian為重度憂鬱。

She was diagnosed with having diabetes.

她被診斷為糖尿病。

diagnosis (n.) 診斷

例句：

What is the diagnosis?

診斷是什麼？

The doctor has made an initial diagnosis.

醫師已經做了初步的診斷。

treatment (n.) 治療

例句：

Her sister was undergoing a treatment for breast cancer.

她姐姐正在進行乳癌治療。

The patient is responding well to the treatment.

病人對於治療的反應良好。

injection (n.) 注射

例句：

Daily insulin injections are necessary for some diabetics.

有些糖尿病患(diabetic)必須每天注射胰島素。

You'll need to have some injections before you go to the Amazon.

你去亞馬遜河探險之前必須注射一些疫苗。

operation (n.) 手術

詞彙：

a stomach/heart operation 胃部／心臟手術

例句：

I'll ask the surgeon when he can fit you in for an operation.

我會問外科醫師什麼時候能幫你安排手術。

The baby needs an operation on the heart, and it will be carried out by an experienced surgeon.

這個嬰兒需要動心臟手術，而手術將由一位經驗豐富的醫生來執行。

prescription (n.) 處方

詞彙：

a doctor's prescription 醫師處方

例句：

These drugs are only available on prescription.

這些藥只能透過醫師處方取得。

The doctor gave me a prescription for antibiotics.

醫生開給我一些抗生素(antibiotics)。

pharmacy (n.) 藥局

(英式英語有時候會用：chemist)

例句：

There is an all-night pharmacy around the corner.

轉角處有間徹夜營業的藥局。

painkiller (n.) 止痛藥

例句：

The body produces chemicals which are natural painkillers.

人體會自己製造化學物質，而這些化學物質就像是天然的止痛劑。

tablet (n.) 藥錠、藥片

詞彙：

indigestion/antidepressant/sleeping/

vitamin tablets

促進消化／鎮定／安眠／維他命的藥錠

two tablets of aspirin 兩片阿斯匹靈

例句：

Take one tablet three times a day after meals.

三餐飯後服用一錠，一天三次。

pill (n.) 藥丸、藥片

詞彙：

sleeping/vitamin pill 安眠藥／維他命錠

例句：

The doctor gave me some pills for the pain.

醫生開了止痛藥錠給我。

特殊：

the pill 指婦女日常使用的避孕藥

例句：

Are you on the pill?

妳有在服用避孕藥嗎？

Caroline had to come off the pill when she developed medical problems.

Caroline停止服用避孕藥，因為它衍生出一些健康上的問題。

capsule (n.) 膠囊

例句：

Take one capsule three times a day.

每天三次，每次服用一顆膠囊。

ointment (n.) 藥膏

例句：

Apply this ointment to your hand.

將藥膏塗抹在你的手上。

MP3 029

side effect (n.) 副作用

例句：

The treatment has no significant side effects.

這個治療沒有什麼顯著的副作用。

Does this drug have any side effects?

請問這個藥有沒有什麼副作用？

形容人：外表

Describing People: Appearances

MP3 030

頭髮：

long (adj.) 長的

詞彙：

long hair 長髮

short (adj.) 短的

詞彙：

short hair 短髮

shoulder-length (adj.) 及肩的

詞彙：

shoulder-length hair 及肩長髮

bald (adj.) 禿頭

片語：

go bald (lose hair) 掉髮

例句：

He started going bald in his twenties.

他從二十幾歲開始禿頭。

He is bald.

他禿頭。

curly (adj.) 捲曲的、捲(髮)

詞彙：

curly red hair 紅色的鬈髮

例句：

Vivian has blond, curly hair.

Vivian有一頭金色的鬈髮。

straight (adj.) 直的、直(髮)

詞彙：

straight hair 直髮

例句：

He has got long, straight hair.

他有一頭長直髮。

lank (adj.)
(未經整理的、沒有吸引力的）直髮

詞彙：

lank hair 直髮

wavy (adj.) 波浪狀的

詞彙：

wavy hair 波浪狀的頭髮

例句：

Sarah has got lovely wavy red hair.

Sarah有一頭迷人的紅卷髮。

髮型：

bangs/fringe (n.) 瀏海

(美式用法為bangs；英式用法為fringe)

詞彙：

a short fringe/short bangs 短瀏海

例句：

My fringe needs cutting.

我的瀏海需要修剪。

cornrow (n.) 辮子頭、玉米鬚頭

例句：

Manny Ramirez likes his hair in cornrows, but braiding it takes a long time.

Manny(知名的棒球選手)喜歡辮子頭的造型，但綁辮子卻很耗時。

MP3 032

part/parting (n.) 分、分流
(美式用法為part；英式用法為parting)

詞彙：

a side part/parting 旁分

a center part/a centre parting 中分

例句：

Emma has straight, shoulder-length hair, a side part, and short bangs.

Emma留著一頭及肩、旁分的直髮，還帶有短短的瀏海。

bun (n.) 髻，包頭

sideburns (n.) 鬢角

ponytail (n.) 馬尾

crew cut (n.) 平頭

Afro (n.) 爆炸頭

Bob cut (n.) 鮑伯頭

plait/braid (n./v.) 辮子（綁辮子）

美式用法為plait；英式用法為braid

highlight (n./v.) 挑染

例句：

Maria's hair is dark brown with pink highlights.

Maria的頭髮是深棕色帶些粉色挑染。

extension (n.) 接髮

例句：

Lisa Salon offers the best quality of hair extension service in this town.

Lisa沙龍提供鎮裡最好的接髮服務。

MP3 033

髮色：

grey (adj.) 斑白的

例句：

He used to have black hair but now it has gone grey, and even almost white.

他曾經滿頭黑髮，但如今髮色已經轉斑白，幾乎全部變白了。

auburn (adj.) 棕紅色

例句：

He is auburn-haired.

他的頭髮是紅棕色的。

blonde/fair (adj.) 金色

red (adj.) 紅色

brown (adj.) 棕色

ginger (adj.) 薑黃色

black (adj.) 黑色

chestnut (n.) 栗子色

brunette (n./adj.) 棕髮的(女生)

brunet (n./adj.) 棕髮的(男生)

burgundy (adj.) 酒紅色

flaxen (adj.) 亞麻色

dip-dyed (adj.) 漸層染的

dip-dyed hair (n.) 漸層染髮

MP3 034

臉型：

thin (adj.) 細長的

詞彙：

thin face (n.)/thin-faced (adj.) 細長的臉

例句：

He has got a thin face.

他有張細長的臉。

round (adj.) 圓的

詞彙：

round face (n.)/round-faced (adj.) 圓臉

oval (adj.) 鵝蛋(臉)

例句：

She has an oval face.

她有張鵝蛋臉。

square (adj.) 方的(臉)，國字(臉)

例句：

He has a square jaw.

他有個方下巴。

chubby (adj.) 胖呼呼的

例句：

The baby has cute, chubby cheeks.

這個寶寶有張可愛、胖呼呼的臉龐。

MP3 035

臉部特徵：

cheekbone (n.) 顴骨、頰骨

例句：

Jasmine has a thin face with high cheekbones.

Jasmine有張削瘦而顴骨凸出的臉。

dimple (n.) 酒窩

例句：

She is a child with blonde, curly hair, blue eyes, and dimples.

她是個有著金色捲髮、藍眼，還有酒窩的孩子。

freckle (n.) 雀斑（在使用時多為複數，不太可能只有一個雀斑）

例句：

He has red hair and freckles.

他有一頭紅髮和雀斑。

wrinkle (n.) 皺紋（在使用時多為複數，不太可能只有一條皺紋）

詞彙：

anti-wrinkle cream 除(抗)皺霜

例句：

There are few wrinkles around her eyes.

她的雙眼周圍有些細紋。

moustache (n.) 髭（嘴唇上的短鬚）

例句：

My father has a thick, black moustache.

我爸爸留了一嘴又粗又黑的髭。

MP3 036

beard (n.) 鬍（下巴上的毛髮）

片語：

shave off one's beard 刮鬍子

例句：

John shaved off his beard but kept his moustache.

John剃掉了他的鬍子，但保留了嘴上的髭。

scar (n.) 傷疤

例句：

Nick has a small scar on his jaw.

Nick的下巴上有一道小傷疤。

spot (n.) 痣

例句：

Marilyn Monroe had a spot on her cheek.

Marilyn Monroe（1926-62, 美國知名影星）的臉頰上有顆痣。

身形：

tall (adj.) 高的

例句：

Eric is young and tall.

Eric又高又年輕。

She is only 5 feet tall.

她只有五呎高。

short (adj.) 矮的

例句：

I'm quite short but my father is very tall.

我雖然挺矮的，但我父親很高。

slim (adj.) 苗條的（正面意涵）

例句：

Iris is short and slim, with light brown hair and blue eyes.

Iris很瘦小，有著淺棕色的頭髮和藍色的眼睛。

skinny (adj.) 瘦的（負面意涵）

例句：

Nadia should eat more. She is much too skinny.

Nadia實在太瘦了，應該多吃一些。

thin (adj.) 瘦的

例句：

Peter is thin and very tall.

Peter很瘦，而且非常高。

plump/stout/overweight (adj.) 肥胖的（直接說fat並不禮貌）

詞彙：

a short, plump woman 一個矮胖的女士

例句：

Kevin is a rather plump man.

Kevin還蠻胖的。

I used to be very overweight.

我曾經超重許多。

muscular (adj.) 肌肉發達的

例句：

He wished he were more muscular.

他希望自己更強壯些。

tattoo (n.) 刺青、紋身

詞彙：

a tattoo of a snake 蛇形紋身

形容詞：

MP3 038

tattooed (adj.) 被紋身的、刺青的

例句：

The Maori's face was heavily tattooed.

毛利人的臉佈滿了刺青。

stay in shape (v. phr.) 身材保持良好

例句：

Kenny works out regularly in order to stay in shape.

Kenny為了保持良好身材，規律地健身。

shapely (adj.) 身材曼妙的

medium build (n. phr.) 中等身材的

例句：

Olive is of medium build.

Olive身材中等。

整體印象：

handsome (adj.) 英俊的

例句：

Sam is tall, dark, and handsome.

Sam很高、黝黑，而且英俊。

beautiful (adj.) 美麗的

例句：

Her mother was a beautiful woman.

她的母親曾經是個大美女。

pretty (adj.) 漂亮的

例句：

He has a very pretty wife.

他娶了一個漂亮老婆。

good-looking (adj.) 漂亮的、迷人的

例句：

Mary is a very good-looking young lady.

Mary是個非常漂亮的小姑娘。

ugly (adj.) 醜陋的

filthy (adj.) 骯髒猥瑣的

well-built (adj.) 身材壯的

well-proportioned (adj.) 身材比例好的

disabled (adj.) 殘障的

blind (adj.) 眼盲的

deaf (adj.) 耳聾的

dumb (adj.) 啞的

crippled (adj.) 殘障的、跛腳的

形容人：特質

Describing People:Characterisitics

MP3 040

形容一個人的聰明才智：

intelligent (adj.) 聰明、有見地（可以形容人，也可以形容事物）

詞彙：

an intelligent young man 一個聰明的年輕人

an intelligent remark/comment

一個有見地的意見或評論

例句：

Surely an intelligent person like you can deal with this problem.

像你這麼聰明的人一定能解決這個問題。

bright (adj.) 聰明的

例句：

Bill is one of the brightest students in the class.

Bill是班上最聰明的學生之一。

clever (adj.)

聰明的、伶俐的、機巧的

(可以形容人，也可以形容事物)

例句：

Michael has never been very clever, but he tries hard.

Michael雖不聰明，但他很努力。

Fiona has a clever idea for getting us out of our present difficulties.

Fiona有個妙點子能讓我們擺脫當前的困境。

gifted (adj.)

天資聰穎的、在某方面極具天賦的

詞彙：

MP3 041

a gifted dancer/musician/pianist/athlete

有天份的舞者／音樂家／鋼琴演奏家／運動員

例句：

Schools often fail to cater for the needs of gifted children.

學校教育通常無法滿足資優兒童的需求。

talented (adj.) 極具天賦的

詞彙：

a talented designer 極具天賦的設計師

例句：

Emma Watson is a talented young actress.

Emma Watson（英國知名女演員）是個有天份的年輕演員。

smart (adj.) 聰明的（可以形容人，也可以形容事物）

例句：

Sophie is a smart, hard-working student.

Sophie是個聰明又上進的學生。

Taking the elevator when the building catches fire is not a smart move.

在建築物失火時搭乘電梯不是個聰明的舉動。

knowledgeable (adj.)

對某方面知識淵博的、涉獵甚深的

例句：

Jason is extremely knowledgeable about classical music.

Jason對於古典音樂有深厚的素養。

sophisticated (adj.) 成熟的；人情練達的

例句：

The first lady is elegant and sophisticated.

總統夫人既優雅又老練得體。

stupid/foolish/silly/brainless (adj.)

愚蠢的、笨的（較不禮貌）

例句：

I did not ask because I was afraid of looking stupid.

我沒問是因為我害怕那樣做會顯得我很蠢。

Steve admits that he made a foolish mistake.

Steve坦承他犯了一個愚蠢的過錯。

It was silly of you to go out in the sun without a hat.

你真蠢，在艷陽下外出居然不戴帽子。

What sort of brainless idiot would do that?

究竟是怎樣的蠢蛋才會搞出這個名堂？

形容一個人的態度：

polite (adj.) 有禮貌的

(可以形容人，也可以形容事物)

例句：

Ken is always so polite to people.

Ken對人總是彬彬有禮。

Mary forced a polite smile.

Mary硬是擠出禮貌性的微笑。

rude (adj.) 粗魯的、無禮的

(可以形容人，也可以形容事物)

詞彙：

a rude word/joke/gesture

無禮的、冒犯的字眼／笑話／姿勢(手勢)

例句：

MP3 043

It's rude not to say "Thank you" when you are given something.

當你從別人那拿到東西時，不道謝是很沒有禮貌的。

I don't want to seem rude, but I'd rather be alone.

我並不想無禮，但我想要一個人靜一靜。

optimistic (adj.) 樂觀的
(可以形容人，也可以形容事物)

例句：

An optimistic person (an optimist) always looks on the bright side.

樂觀的人(樂觀主義者)總是看著光明面。

The sixties were, in general, an optimistic decade.

六〇年代的時代氛圍整體來說是樂觀的。

pessimistic (adj.) 悲觀的
(可以形容人，也可以形容事物)

例句：

A pessimistic person (a pessimist) always expects the worst to happen.

悲觀的人(悲觀主義者)總是期待最壞的事情發生。

The tone of the meeting was very pessimistic.

會議的整體氛圍非常悲觀。

broad-minded/open-minded (adj.)

開明的、心胸開闊的、願意接受意見或新事物的

片語：

be open-minded about 對…抱持著開放的態度

例句：

Lisa is open-minded enough to consider all new ideas.

Lisa的胸襟開闊，很願意接受新概念。

Nowadays, doctors tend to be more open-minded about alternative treatments.

現代的醫生對於另類療法已能抱持相對開放的態度。

narrow-minded (adj.)

封閉的、不開明的、偏執的，氣量狹小的

詞彙：

a narrow-minded view/opinion

偏狹的論點／意見

例句：

I can't get along with those narrow-minded people.

我沒辦法和那些偏執的人相處。

sympathetic (adj.) 富有同情心的

詞彙：

a sympathetic ear

一個富有同情心、並且願意聆聽的人

例句：

You are not being very sympathetic.

你不是很有同情心。

If you need a sympathetic ear, I am always available.

如果你想找一個富有同情心的對象傾訴，可以找我。

considerate (adj.) 體貼的、善解人意的

例句：

Diana is a considerate boss who is always willing to listen.

Diana是個體貼的上司，總是願意傾聽。

It is very considerate of you to include me.

你真體貼，有算我一份。

MP3 045

thoughtful (adj.)

貼心的、替人著想的、樂於助人的

例句：

It is very thoughtful of you to remember my birthday.

你好貼心，居然記得我的生日。

self-centered/selfish (adj.)

自私的、自我為中心的

詞彙：

a spoiled, selfish kid

一個被寵壞的、自私的孩子

例句：

How can you be so selfish?

你怎麼可以這麼自私？

kind (adj.)

仁慈的、和藹的、富有同情心的、樂於助人的

例句：

Amy is a very kind and thoughtful person who always helps others.

Amy是個仁慈而貼心的人，總是樂於幫助別人。

cruel (adj.) 殘酷的、冷血的、惡毒的

詞彙：

a cruel sense of humor 惡毒的幽默

例句：

How could you be so cruel to someone who didn't even know you?

你怎麼可以對一個素昧平生的人這麼殘忍？

MP3 046

genererous (adj.) 慷慨的、大方的

例句：

Oprah Winfrey is clearly a generous and warm person. She does a lot of work for charity.

Oprah (美國知名主持人)顯然是個溫暖又慷慨的人。她從事許多慈善事業。

thrifty (adj.)

勤儉的、節省的（正面、中庸特質）

例句：

My grandmother was a thrifty woman.

我的祖母是個勤儉持家的婦人。

They have plenty of money now, but they still tend to be thrifty.

儘管他們現在很富有，但他們還是很儉省。

stingy/mean (adj.) 吝嗇的、小氣的 (負面特質)

例句：

Lisa tries to save money without being stingy.

Lisa努力地在省錢的同時避免成為吝嗇的人。

He is too mean to buy his fiancée a ring.

他小氣到不幫他的未婚妻買只婚戒。

supportive (adj.) 願意支持、鼓勵的

例句：

Children with supportive parents often do better at school than those without.

受到父母親支持和鼓舞的孩子在學校的表現通常比沒有獲得雙親肯定的孩子來得好。

MP3 047

honest/trustworthy/reliable/sincere (adj.)

誠實的、正直的、值得信靠的（可形容人，也可形容事物）

詞彙：

a/an honest/trustworthy/reliable/sincere person/worker

一個正直而值得信靠的人／員工

a sincere apology 真心的道歉

例句：

I'd like you to give me an honest answer.

我期望你給我一個誠實的回應。

Steven is the most experienced and trustworthy guide.

Steven是最經驗老道，也最值得信賴的嚮導。

dishonest/untrustworthy/unreliable/insincere (adj.)

不誠實的、不值得信賴的

詞彙：

an insincere smile/apology

不真心的微笑／道歉

a/an dishonest/untrustworthy/unreliable/insincere person 不誠實、不值得信靠的人

例句：

The newspapers disclosed that there were dishonest officers in the police force.

報紙揭露了警察系統內部有不肖的員警。

active/energetic (adj.)

精力充沛的、充滿活力的

例句：

Mrs. Brown is over 80 but remains very active.

Brown太太已經八十多歲了，但依舊活力四射。

Nancy is an energetic young lady.

Nancy是個活力十足的年輕女孩。

outgoing/extroverted/sociable (adj.)

外向的、活潑的

詞彙：

an outgoing/extroverted personality

外向的、活潑的個性

例句：

Sales representatives need to be outgoing because they are constantly meeting customers.

業務代表必須是外向的人，因為他們得經常面對客戶。

Mr. and Mrs. Smith are a very pleasant, sociable couple.

Smith夫婦是一對非常外向、好相處的夫妻。

shy/introverted (adj.)

內向的、害羞的、不善交際的

詞彙：

an introverted/ a shy child

一個內向、害羞的孩子

例句：

It is strange that one of the twins is so extroverted while the other is so introverted.

奇怪的是，這對雙胞胎一個很外向一個很內向。

Children are often shy with people they don't know.

孩子在陌生人面前經常感到害羞。

easy-going/relaxed/laid-back (adj.)

隨和的、放鬆的、淡定的、從容的，不容易緊張或被激怒的

詞彙：

an easy-going/a relaxed/laid-back attitude

輕鬆的、寫意的態度

a friendly, easy-going type of guy

一個友善、隨和的人

例句：

I've never seen Lonnie worried or anxious in any way – she's so laid-back.

我從來沒見過Lonnie著急或焦慮。她實在很淡定從容！

sensitive (adj.)

敏感的、多愁善感的、情緒化的

片語：

be sensitive to 對…很敏感。很容易被刺激、挑起情緒

例句：

I didn't realize that she was so sensitive to criticism.

我不曉得她對於批評的反應會如此激烈。

reasonable/sensible (adj.)

理性的、明智的、實際的

詞彙：

a reasonable/sensible option

一個明智的選擇

a reasonable/sensible man

一個理智的人

例句：

I don't think any sensible person could agree with him.

我不覺得任何一個有理智的人會同意他。

determined (adj.)

果斷的、果決的、意志堅定的（正面特質）

詞彙：

a determined person 意志堅定、堅持到底的人

stubborn (adj.)

頑固、倔強、堅持己見的

(和determined近似，但較有負面意涵)

例句：

Vincent is as stubborn as a mule.

Vincent就像騾子一樣頑固。

self-confident (adj.) 自信的

例句：

I remember that Jack was popular and self-confident at school.

我記得Jack在學校時有自信又受歡迎。

bold (adj.) 大膽的、無畏的

(可形容人，也可形容事物)

詞彙：

a bold move/step/statement

一個大膽的舉動／步驟／聲明

例句：

Both Abraham Lincoln and Winston Churchill are bold leaders.

林肯(解放黑奴的美國總統)和邱吉爾(二戰時的英國首相)都是無畏的領袖。

timid (adj.) 膽小的、羞怯的 (可形容人，也可形容事物)

詞彙：

a timid smile 羞怯的微笑

例句：

Lucy is a rather timid child.

Lucy是個蠻膽小羞怯的孩子。

The government took a policy that is both timid and inadequate.

政府採取了一個既膽小又不恰當的策略。

051

arrogant (adj.)

傲慢的、自大的、自負的

例句：

How arrogant of her to say that!

她竟然傲慢到說出這種話！

ambitious (adj.)

雄心勃勃的、有野心的

(可形容人，也可形容事物)

詞彙：

an ambitious young politician

雄心勃勃的年輕政客

an ambitious aim/plan

有野心的、挑戰性很高的目標／計劃

pushy (adj.)

為達目標不擇手段的、緊迫盯人的

（負面特質）

詞彙：

a pushy salesman 無所不用其極的銷售員

pushy parents 緊迫盯人的父母

bossy (adj.)

跋扈的、頤指氣使的、愛指揮別人的

（負面特質）

例句：

Nadia moved out because her mother-in-law was too bossy.

Nadia搬出去住因為她的婆婆太愛指使人。

patient (adj.) 有耐心的

片語：

be patient with 對…有耐心

例句：

It's difficult to be patient when you're stuck in a long queue.

當深陷在一條長長的隊伍之中時，你很難保持耐性。

My school teacher is always very patient with me.

我的老師總是對我很有耐心。

impatient (adj.) 沒有耐心的、性急的

片語：

impatient with 對…失去耐性

例句：

Jack gets impatient with people when they don't agree with him.

當別人不同意Jack的時候，他很快就會失去耐性。

The customers are growing impatient with the lack of results.

因為等不到結果，顧客們逐漸失去耐性。

教育

Education

MP3 053

學制和學位：educational system and degrees

kindergarten (n.) 幼稚園
(英式英語：nursery school)

elementary school (n.) 小學
(英式英語：primary school)

junior high school (n.) 國中
(英式英語：secondary school)

senior high school (n.) 高中
(英式英語：secondary school)

college (n.) 大學中的學院、大學、高等職業學校(英)

例句：

Emily graduated from the university's College of Business Management.

Emily畢業於這間大學的商業管理學院。

Karl took a year off before going to college.

Karl在上大學前休了一年的假。(英式英語中稱這一年叫：gap year)

university (n.) 大學

例句：

Teresa applied to six universities and was accepted by all of them.

Teresa申請了六所大學並且全都被錄取了。

undergraduate (n.) 大學生

詞彙：

a second-year undergraduate 一個大二生

MP3 054

freshman (adj./n.)

大一新生(的)、新鮮人

詞彙：

freshman year 大一那一年

sophomore (adj./n.) 大二生

例句：

My son is in his sophomore year.

我兒子目前大二。

junior (adj./n.) 大三生(的)

詞彙：

junior year 大三那一年

senior (adj./n.) 大四生(的)

例句：

My sister will be a senior this year.

我妹妹今年即將升大四。

department (n.) 科系、系所

詞彙：

department of history 歷史系

graduate school (n.) 研究所
(英式用語：postgraduate education)

例句：

Most graduate schools require their students to write and defend a thesis or dissertation.

多數的研究所會要求學生撰寫論文和參加論文口試。

graduate (n.) 畢業生、研究生
(英式用法：postgraduate)

詞彙：

MP3 0055

a Yale graduate/a graduate of Yale

耶魯的畢業生

例句：

Barack Obama is a graduate of Harvard Law School.

Obama(美國總統)是哈佛法學院的畢業生。

degree (n.) 學位

詞彙：

a biology degree 生物學學位

bachelor's degree 大學學位

master's degree 碩士學位

a master's degree in English literature

英語文學的碩士學位

例句：

Emma is doing a degree at Oxford University.

Emma正在牛津大學攻讀學位。

doctorate (n.) 博士學位

(PhD: Doctor of Philosophy)

例句：

He was awarded a doctorate in mathematics.

他曾經獲頒數學博士學位。

Lisa has a PhD in English literature.

Lisa擁有英語文學的博士學位。

MP3 056

校園生活：

school (n.) 學校

詞彙：

school bus 校車

片語：

attend school/go to school 上學

例句：

Which school do you attend?

你讀哪間學校？

My father used to pick me up from school.

我父親以前會去學校接我下課。

campus (n.) 校園

片語：

on/off campus 校內／校外

例句：

We have accommodation for 200 students on campus.

我們有容納200名學生的校內宿舍。

There is a website offering information about off-campus housing for students.

有個網站專門提供學生校外租屋的資訊。

library (n.) 圖書館

詞彙：

a public library 公設圖書館

a library book 一本圖書館的書

playground (n.) 遊樂場

例句：

The students are playing on the playground.

學生們在遊樂場玩耍。

laboratory (n.) 實驗室

詞彙：

laboratory assistant 實驗室助理

laboratory equipment 試驗設備、實驗器材

textbook (n.) 教科書

詞彙：

a science textbook 科學課本

an accounting textbook 會計學課本

school uniform (n.) 校服、制服

例句：

Paul is still wearing his school uniform.

Paul仍舊穿著他的校服。

register (v.) 註冊、登記、登錄

例句：

I register the car in my name.

這輛車登記在我的名下。

Students have to register for the new course by the end of April.

學生必須在四月底前註冊新課程。

enroll (v.) 登記、加入、列名

片語：

enroll for/in a course/program/workshop

加入、列名(某課程)

enroll at a school/college/university 入學

例句：

I enrolled in a training program for project manager.

我報名了一個專案經理的培訓計劃。

MP3 058

tuition (n.) 學費

例句：

Tuition increased by 10% universities this year.

今年的大學學費漲幅達10%。

scholarship (n.) 獎學金

片語：

award someone a scholarship 給予某人獎學金

win/gain/receive a scholarship 獲得獎學金

例句：

Paula was awarded a scholarship to attend Yale University.

Paula獲得獎學金就讀耶魯大學。

Emily went to the Royal College of Music on a scholarship.

Emily以獎學金生的身份就讀Royal College of Music

（皇家音樂學院）。

student loan (n.) 就學貸款

片語：

take out a student loan 申辦就學貸款

classroom (n.) 教室

例句：

Students majoring in biology spend two days each week in a lab and four days in the classroom.

主修生物的學生一週花兩天在實驗室，剩下四天在教室上課。

teacher (n.) 老師

詞彙：

history/science/English teacher

歷史／科學／英文老師

MP3 059

professor (n.) 教授

詞彙：

biology/French professor 生物／法文教授

例句：

My father is a professor of Chinese.

我父親是個中文教授。

student (n.) 學生

詞彙：

law/medical/engineering student

法學院／醫科／電機系的學生

exchange student 交換學生

student teacher/nurse

實習教師／實習護士

例句：

Tom is a second-year student at the University of York.

湯姆是約克大學二年級的學生。

pupil (n.) 學童、學徒

例句：

The school has over 500 pupils.

這個學校有超過500名學童。

class (n.)

片語：

miss/skip/cut a class 蹺課

（正式用法：miss deliberately）

例句：

If you often miss classes deliberately, you probably will not get good grades.

如果你經常蹺課，你大概不會拿到好成績。

MP3 060

course (n.) 課程

片語：

do/take a course 修課

offer/run a course 開課

drop a course 退選、棄修

例句：

The school runs an introductory course in economics.

這間學校有開經濟學的入門課程。

program (n.) 課程、學程 (英式英語：programme)

例句：

A course covers a single subject, while a program usually contains many courses and leads to a certificate or diploma.

一門課通常涵蓋一個特別的主題；而一個學程通常會

有好幾門課，並且提供文憑。

lecture (n.) 以講授為主的課；演講

例句：

Professor Jordan will give us a lecture on Italian art.

Jordan教授將要講授一門有關義大利藝術的課。

seminar (n.)
小班制的專題討論課、小型的討論會

詞彙：

seminar room 研討室、會議室

例句：

I attended a seminar on environmental protection.

我參加了一個以環保為主題的研討會。

0
6
1

tutorial (n.) 一對一或小班制的課

詞彙：

a tutorial system

師徒制、一對一的教學體系

major (n./v.)

主修；主修

片語：

major in　主修

例句：

Ann majored in philosophy at Stanford/Ann's major at Stanford is philosophy.

Ann在Stanford大學時的主修是哲學。

What is your major, history or philosophy?

你的主修是什麼？歷史還是哲學？

Sherry was a political science major at an Ivy League college.

Sherry在某常春藤聯盟的大學中主修政治學。

credit (n.) 學分

例句：

This course counts as three credits towards his degree.

這門課在他的畢業學分中佔三學分。

academic year (n.) 學年

例句：

An academic year usually starts in autumn and ends in summer.

一學年通常始於秋天並在夏天結束。

term (n.) 學期（英式英語較常使用）

詞彙：

term time 學期中

MP3 062

autumn/spring/summer term

秋季、春季、夏季班（英國一年的三個學期）

例句：

What classes are you taking this term?

這學期你修哪些課？

semester (n.) 學期（美式和澳洲英語）

例句：

In the US, there are two semesters in an academic year.

在美國，一學年有兩個學期。

examination (n.) 考試
(通常會用簡寫exam表示)

片語：

take/do/sit an exam 參加考試

pass/fail an exam 通過／沒通過考試

resit an exam 重考（英式英語較常使用）

do well/do badly in an exam 考得好／考得差

例句：

If you fail the exam, you can resit it next year.

要是你這次沒通過考試，你可以明年再重考。

assignment (n.) 作業、功課

例句：

I have a lot of reading assignments to complete before the end of term.

期末前我有好多閱讀作業要消化。

essay (n.) 小論文、論說文

例句：

MP3 063

For homework, Professor Lin asked his students to write an essay on/ about global warming.

林教授要求他的學生寫一篇有關全球暖化的小論文作為回家功課。

thesis (n.) 學位論文

例句：

Amanda wrote a doctoral thesis on social security.

Amanda寫了一篇探討社會福利的博士論文。

mark (n./v.) 分數、打分數（英式英語較常使用）

例句：

What was Sam's mark on the last history test?

Sam上次的歷史考試考幾分？

The teacher spent all night marking exam papers.

這位老師花了一整晚閱卷。

grade (n.) 分數、等第

片語：

get/gain/obtain a grade 取得成績

例句：

Ethan never studies, but he always obtains good grades.

雖然Ethan都不讀書，但他總能取得好成績。

只要會這些就夠英文單字

ESSENTIAL WORDS FOR EVERYDAY USE

MP3 064

人際關係

Human Relationships

家庭：

family (n.) 家人
（後頭可加單數或複數的動詞形式）

例句：

We ought to help David. After all, he is family.

我們應該協助David，畢竟他是我們的家人。

relative (n.) 親戚

詞彙：

blood relative 血親

close/distant relative 近／遠親

例句：

We spent the weekend visiting relatives.

我們在週末探訪親戚。

I haven't got many blood relatives.

我沒有很多血親。

parent (n.) 雙親
(單數時表示父親或母親)

詞彙：

single parent 單親

single-parent family 單親家庭

（或**one-parent family**）

birth parent 生父／生母

例句：

Has Amanda met your parents yet?

Amanda見過你的父母了嗎？

dad/father (n.) 父親

詞彙：

real/natural father 生父

single father 單親爸爸

stepfather 繼父

例句：

The thought of becoming a father terrified Tom.

即將為人父的想法嚇壞了Tom。

mom/mum/mother (n.) 母親

詞彙：

birth mother 生母

single mother 單親媽媽

stepmother 繼母

an expectant mother/a mother-to-be

一個孕婦

例句：

She is like a mother to me.

她就像是我媽。

child (n.) 孩子（children複數）

詞彙：

only child 獨子

片語：

have a child/have children 懷孕

例句：

Adoption is an option for the couples who can't have children.

對無法生育的夫妻而言，領養(adoption)是個選項。

I'm the middle child in our family.

我是家裡排行中間的孩子。

son (n.) 兒子

詞彙：

stepson 繼子

MP3 066

daughter (n.) 女兒

詞彙：

stepdaughter 繼女

brother (n.) 兄弟

詞彙：

older brother 哥哥

younger brother 弟弟

big brother 大哥

baby brother 小弟

half-brother 同父異母或同母異父的兄弟

stepbrother

繼父與前妻所生的男孩

或繼母與前夫所生的男孩

brother-in-law 妻子或丈夫(伴侶)的兄弟

sister (n.) 姐妹

詞彙：

older sister 姐姐

younger sister 妹妹

big sister 大姐

baby sister 小妹

half-sister 同父異母或同母異父的姐妹

stepsister

繼父與前妻所生的女孩

或繼母與前夫所生的女孩

sister-in-law 妻子或丈夫(伴侶)的姐妹

sibling (n.) 兄弟姐妹、手足

例句：

I have four siblings, three sisters and one brother.

我有四位手足，三個姐姐一個哥哥。

MP3 067

cousin (n.) 堂、表兄弟姐妹

詞彙：

distant cousin 遠房堂／表兄弟姐妹

例句：

Jack and I are cousins.

Jack和我是堂／表兄弟。

maternal (adj.) 母系的、母親的

詞彙：

maternal grandmother 外婆、母親的母親

maternal relatives 母系的親戚

例句：

Kevin's maternal grandmother is still alive.

Kevin的外婆依舊健在。

paternal (adj.) 父系的

詞彙：

paternal grandmother 祖母、父親的母親

grandparent (n.) 祖父母

grandfather (n.) 祖父

grandmother (n.) 祖母

grandchild (n.) 孫子或孫女
(grandchildren複數)

grandson (n.) 孫子

granddaughter (n.) 孫女

great-grandparent (n.)
曾祖父母、爸爸或媽媽的祖父母

great-grandfather (n.) 曾祖父

great-grandmother (n.) 曾祖母

great-grandchild (n.) 曾孫
(great-grandchildren複數)

great-grandson (n.) 曾孫

great-granddaughter (n.) 曾孫女

uncle (n.) 叔叔伯伯舅舅
(父母親的兄弟)，
或者是姑姑阿姨的老公

aunt (n.) 姑姑阿姨(父母親的姐妹)，
或者是叔叔伯伯舅舅的老婆

nephew (n.) 外甥、姪子

niece (n.) 外甥女、姪女

marriage (n.) 婚姻

片語：

by marriage 因為婚姻、隨著婚姻而來

例句：

Miranda has a son by her first marriage.

Miranda在第一次婚姻中有了一個兒子。

I'm related to Bill by marriage.

我和Bill是姻親。(因為婚姻而產生的親屬關係)

spouse (n.) 配偶、另一半

例句：

In 60 percent of the households surveyed, both spouses went out to work.

在被訪問的家戶(household)中，夫妻倆都外出上班的佔了百分之六十。

wife (n.) 老婆、妻子

詞彙：

ex-wife 前妻

wife-to-be 未婚妻

片語：

pronounce someone man and wife/

pronounce someone husband and wife

宣佈結為夫妻

例句：

MP3 069

The judge pronounced them man and wife.

法官宣佈他們結為夫妻。

husband (n.) 老公、丈夫

詞彙：

ex-husband 前夫

husband-to-be 未婚夫

house husband 家庭主(煮)夫

father-in-law (n.) 公公、岳父

mother-in-law (n.) 婆婆、岳母

son-in-law (n.) 女婿、女兒的老公

daughter-in-law (n.) 媳婦、兒子的老婆

親密關係：

single (adj./n.) 單身、單身的人

詞彙：

a single woman/man/person

單身的女人／男人／單身者

singles night 單身之夜(注意此時singles為複數)

例句：

They attended the singles night at a club.

他們參加一個夜店舉辦的單身之夜。

date (v.) 約會、交往

例句：

My wife and I dated for three years before we got married.

我和我太太交往三年才結婚。

070

see (v.) 約會、交往

片語：

be seeing someone 和某人交往

例句：

Do you know whether she's seeing anyone at the moment?

你知道她現在有在和誰交往嗎？

together (adv.) 交往、在一起

片語：

get together 交往

get back together 復合

例句：

Amanda and James have been together now for almost three years.

Amanda和James已經交往三年了。

When did Janice and Steve get back together?

Janice和Steve什麼時候復合的？

boyfriend (n.) 男友

詞彙：

a steady boyfriend 長期交往的男友

ex-boyfriend 前男友

girlfriend (n.) 女友

詞彙：

a steady girlfriend 長期、固定交往的女友

ex-girlfriend 前女友

partner (n.) 同性或異性的同居伴侶，或同性婚姻中的雙方

詞彙：

life partner 終生伴侶

例句：

MP3 071

Are partners invited to the office party?

這次辦公室聚會有邀請伴侶參加嗎？

live together/cohabit (v.) 同居

詞彙：

cohabiting couples 同居伴侶

例句：

There is an increasing number of couples that are cohabiting.

這年頭，同居伴侶的數字一直在增加。

My parents don't approve of us living together.

我爸媽不同意我們同居。

propose (v.) 求婚

片語：

propose marriage 求婚

例句：

I remember the night your father proposed to me.

我記得你父親向我求婚的那一夜。

engaged (adj.) 訂婚、已有婚約的

例句：

She is engaged to someone she met at work.

她和一位工作上認識的對象訂婚。

fiancé (n.) 未婚夫

fiancée (n.) 未婚妻

wedding (n.) 婚禮

詞彙：

a wedding cake/dress/invitation/present

婚禮蛋糕／婚紗／婚禮請柬／婚禮禮物

wedding ring 結婚戒指

wedding day 結婚日

wedding anniversary 結婚紀念日

例句：

It was my parents' 35th wedding anniversary last week.

上個星期是我父母35周年的結婚紀念日。

We want a quiet wedding.

我們想要一個安靜的婚禮。

bride (n.) 新娘

詞彙：

bride-to-be 待嫁的新娘

new-bride 新嫁娘、剛過門的老婆

例句：

Phil introduced his new bride to us.

Phil介紹他的新婚妻子給我們認識。

bridegroom/groom (n.) 新郎

例句：

The bride and groom walked down the aisle together.

新郎和新娘並肩走下走道。

bridesmaid (n.) 伴娘、女儐相

best man (n.) 伴郎、男儐相

have an affair/extramarital affair 搞外遇、婚外情

例句：

She's having an affair with a married man.

她和一位有婦之夫外遇。

another woman/the other woman (n.) 女性的第三者

MP3 073

例句：

She hated being the other woman, but what could she do?

她恨透了成為第三者，但她又能做什麼呢？

Do you think there's another woman?

你認為有第三者嗎？

the other man (n.) 男性的第三者

break up/split up (v.) 分手 (無論是否有婚約的親密關係都適用)

例句：

She's just broken up with her boyfriend.

她剛和男朋友分手。

Her parents split up a few months ago.

她的雙親在幾個月前分開了。

separate (v.) 分居

形容詞：

separated (adj.)

分居的、形容分居的狀態

例句：

Michael's parents separated when he was five.

Michael的雙親自他五歲起就分居了。

We have been separated for six months.

我們已分居半年。

divorce (v./n.) 離婚

片語：

get a divorce 離婚

形容詞：

divorced (adj.)

離婚的、形容離婚的狀態

詞彙：

MP3 074

a divorced man 離婚的男人

例句：

She is divorcing her husband.

她正在和丈夫辦離婚。

Divorce is on the increase.

離婚正在增加。

Are you married, single, or divorced?

請問你是已婚、未婚，還是已離婚？(詢問婚姻狀態)

社會：

friend (n.) 朋友

詞彙：

close/good/great friend 好朋友、親密的朋友

best friend 最要好的朋友

old friend 老朋友，相識很久的朋友

friend of the family/family friend

家族的朋友、世交

mutual friend 共同朋友

circle of friends 朋友圈

片語：

make friends 交朋友

例句：

Peter and Nadia met through a mutual friend.

Peter和Nadia是透過共同朋友認識的。

MP3 075

I've made a lot of friends in this job.

我因為這份工作認識很多朋友。

Lisa is very friendly and sociable. She has a wide circle of friends.

Lisa既友善又善於社交。她擁有一個龐大的朋友圈。

roommate (n.) 室友、樓友
(英式英語flatmate/housemate)

例句：

Vincent is moving out next month, so we're looking for another roommate to share the house.

Vincent即將於下個月遷出，所以我們正在找新的室友。

neighbor (n.) 鄰居
(英式英語neighbour)

詞彙：

next-door neighbor 隔壁鄰居

例句：

We have been good neighbors for years.

我們是好幾年的好鄰居。

colleague/workmate (n.) 同事

例句：

It's something that my colleagues at the embassy are extremely concerned with.

這正是我在大使館的同事高度關心的事。

I went out for a drink with a few workmates.

我和一些同事去喝一杯。

employer (n.) 雇主、老闆

例句：

We need a reference from your former employer.

我們需要你前一任雇主的推薦函(reference)。

MP3 076

The university is the largest single employer in the area.

這間大學是這個地區最大的單一雇主。

boss (n.) 老闆

例句：

I started my own business and now I'm my own boss.

我選擇創業。現在的我就是老闆，我為自己工作。

I'll ask my boss if I can have a day off next week.

我要問問我老闆下週我是否能請一天假。

employee (n.) 員工、職員

例句：

She is a former council employee.

她曾經是地方議會的雇員。

client/customer (n.) 客戶

詞彙：

customer services 客服部門

regular customer 常客、老主顧

例句：

Supermarkets use a variety of tactics to attract and retain customers.

超市會用許多策略來吸引和留住顧客。

Mr. Johnson has been a client of this firm for decades.

Mr. Johnson幾十年來都是這家公司的客戶。

acquaintance (n.) 點頭之交

詞彙：

business acquaintance 商業／生意／業務上往來的夥伴(私下並不熟)

例句：

MP3 077

He recognized Mr. Clinton as an old business acquaintance from his years in banking.

他認出Mr. Clinton是他過往在金融業服務時的一個商業夥伴。

stranger (n.) 陌生人

詞彙：

a complete/perfect/total stranger

徹底陌生的人

例句：

People normally do not want to share a room with a complete stranger.

人們一般不願意和陌生人同房。

Children are warned not to talk to strangers.

孩子們被警告別跟陌生人說話。

交通工具

Means of Transportation

078

transportation (n.) 交通、運輸
(英式英語為transport)

詞彙：

public transportation 公共運輸、大眾運輸
(英式英語為**public transport**)

means/mode/form of transportation
交通方式／模式

road transportation/transport
道路運輸、路面運輸

rail transportation/transport 軌道運輸

air transportation/transport 航空運輸

ship transportation/transport 船運

例句：

The price includes hotels and transportation.
這個價錢涵蓋了旅館和交通的費用。

The city needs to improve its public transportation.
這個城市必須加強它的公共運輸系統。

People need to get out of their cars and use other modes of transportation, like cycling.

人們必須捨棄他們的車子並且使用其他如腳踏車等的交通工具。

board (v.) 搭乘（船、巴士、火車、飛機）

片語：

be boarding 開放乘客上機、上船、上車

例句：

Olympic Airways Flight 172 to Istanbul is now boarding at Gate No. 37.

Olympic航空編號172飛往伊斯坦堡的班機(flight)現在在37號閘口開放登機。

Ivy boarded the wrong train.

Ivy搭錯火車(train)了。

MP3 079

passenger (n.) 乘客

詞彙：

airline/rail/car passengers

搭乘航空／鐵路／汽車的旅客

例句：

Two other passengers in the car suffered serious injuries in the accident.

車內另外兩位乘客在事故中受到重傷。

Rail passengers now face even longer delays.

鐵路乘客現在面臨更嚴重的誤點。

ticket (n.) 票

詞彙：

a/an train/bus/airline ticket 火車／公車／飛機票

return/round-trip ticket 來回票

single/one-way ticket 單程票

open ticket 沒有押使用日期的票

例句：

I'd like a return ticket to Sydney, please.

請給我一張去雪梨的來回票。

fare (n.) 交通工具的費用

詞彙：

air/bus/train/taxi fare

機票費用／公車車資／火車票錢／計程車資

half/full fare 半票／全票

excess fare 票價的差額

例句：

Train fares are going up again.

火車票又要漲價了。

If you travel first-class with a second-class ticket, you have to pay the excess fare.

如果你持普通車票搭乘頭等艙(車箱)，你必須補票。

MP3 080

schedule (n.) 時刻表
(英式英文為timetable)

詞彙：

a bus/train schedule/timetable

公車／火車時刻表

on time 準時

例句：

The train was on time.

這輛列車準時。

late/delayed 誤點

詞彙：

seriously/badly delayed 嚴重誤點

slightly delayed 輕微誤點

例句：

The fight was badly delayed because of fog.

航班因為濃霧而嚴重誤點。

This train is always late.

這班火車老是誤點。

cancel (v.) 取消

例句：

The 3:05 train to London has been cancelled.

三點零五分前往倫敦的列車取消了。

depart (v.) 啟程、出發

名詞：

departure (n.) 啟程、出境；

泛指所有啟程的運輸工具

例句：

Our flight departs from Taipei at 6 a.m.

我們的飛機六點從台北起飛。

Dorothy departed for Germany last week.

Dorothy上週啟程去德國。

The next departure for New York will be at 11:00.

前往紐約的下一班車將於11點出發。

arrive (v.) 抵達

名詞：

arrival (n.) 抵達

片語：

arrive at/in 抵達

例句：

What time does your plane arrive?

你的班機幾點到？

The airport monitors show the information of all arrivals and departures.

機場的螢幕顯示所有起降班機的資訊。

destination (n.) 目的地

詞彙：

vacation/holiday/tourist destination

渡假／觀光勝地

例句：

The Caribbean is a popular tourist destination.

加勒比海是很受歡迎的觀光勝地。

We arrived at our destination tired and hungry.

當我們抵達目的地時，又餓又累。

shuttle (n.) 來回接駁的運輸工具（可以是任何形式，像是飛機、火車或巴士）

詞彙：

shuttle bus 接駁公車

例句：

MP3 082

There is a shuttle service between the hotel and the beach.

在飯店和海灘間有定時的接駁服務。

A shuttle bus operates from the city center to the airport.

在市區和機場間有接駁公車提供載客。

passport (n.) 護照

詞彙：

Taiwanese/British/French/American passport

台灣／英國／法國／美國護照

valid passport

合法的、效期內的護照、有效護照

false passport 偽造的護照、假護照

例句：

All people entering the country will need a valid passport.

每一個進入這個國家的人，都必須持有有效護照。

Does David hold an American passport?

David是不是持有美國護照？

She was a German, traveling on a Swiss passport.

她是德國人，旅行時卻用瑞士護照。

visa (n.) 簽證

詞彙：

student/tourist/work visa

學生／觀光／工作簽證

例句：

We traveled to Argentina on a tourist visa.

我們持觀光簽證前往阿根廷旅遊。

The UK recently denied visas to two suspected terrorists.

英國最近拒發簽證給兩個恐怖份子嫌疑人。

MP3 083

baggage (n.) 行李
(英式英語用luggage)

詞彙：

baggage allowance

行李重量許可（行李重量限制）

baggage room/left-luggage office

行李房（寄放行李的地方）

hand luggage/carry-on baggage 手提行李

excess baggage/luggage 過重的行李

例句：

Never leave your luggage unattended.

千萬別讓你的行李離開視線。

How many items of hand luggage am I allowed to take onto the plane?

我可以攜帶幾件手提行李上機？

belongings (n.) 攜帶的物品

詞彙：

personal belongings 個人攜帶的物品

例句：

Remember to take all your personal belongings when you leave.

在你離開前記得帶走你個人所攜帶的物品。

鐵路、地鐵、捷運

084

train (n.) 火車、列車

詞彙：

passenger train 載客列車

freight/goods train 貨運列車

片語：

get on the train 上火車

get off the train 下火車

miss the train 錯過火車

例句：

We travelled across China by train.

我們搭火車在中國四處旅遊。

I took the first train home.

我搭第一班火車回家。

I met her on the train to Boston.

我和她是在開往波士頓的列車上認識的。

subway/underground (n.) 地鐵 (倫敦的地鐵又叫作the Tube)

詞彙：

the New York City Subway 紐約地鐵

the London Underground 倫敦地鐵

例句：

Take the subway to 14th Street.

搭地鐵到第14街！

metro (n.) 捷運

詞彙：

the Paris Metro 巴黎地鐵

the Taipei Metro 台北捷運

(又稱作MRT:

Mass Rapid Transit 大眾快捷運輸系統)

例句：

It'll be quicker to go on the metro.

搭捷運會比較快！

Let's go by metro.

我們搭捷運去！

track (n.) 鐵軌

例句：

Passengers are requested not to walk across the tracks.

旅客被要求不要橫跨鐵軌。

station (n.) 運輸工具暫停好讓旅客上下車的地點

詞彙：

train/rail/railway station 火車站

subway/underground/metro station

地鐵站／捷運站

Grand Central Station 紐約的大中央車站

例句：

We looked on the map to find the nearest subway station.

我們在地圖上尋找最近的地鐵站。

It was dark when we arrived at London Waterloo Station.

當我們抵達倫敦滑鐵盧車站時，天色已晚。

waiting room (n.) 候車室

例句：

Is there a waiting room at the station?

請問車站裡有候車室嗎？

platform (n.) 月台

例句：

The train for Cambridge will depart from platform 9.

往劍橋的火車將從第九月台發車。

He was coming by train, so I waited on the platform.

他坐火車來，所以我在月台上等。

passenger car/coach/carriage (n.) 車箱

例句：

First class accommodation is in the first two coaches.

頭等座位在前兩節車箱。

compartment (n.) 車廂內的小艙房、小隔間

詞彙：

a first-class compartment （火車上的）頭等艙

conductor (n.) 車掌、隨車服務員

例句：

Someone whose job it is to sell tickets on a bus, train, or other public vehicle is called a conductor.

車掌的工作就是在公車、火車，或者是其他大眾運輸上販賣車票。

terminate (v.) 終止服務、到終點站

例句：

This train will terminate at the next stop. Passengers who wish to continue should change trains.

下一站是本列車的終點站。要繼續轉搭乘的旅客請換車。

Trains from Paris terminate at St. Pancras railway station.

來自巴黎的列車終點站都是倫敦的St. Pancras火車站。

main line (n.) 幹線、主線

形容詞：

main-line/mainline (adj.) 主線的

詞彙：

a main line between London and Edinburgh

連接倫敦和愛丁堡的主要鐵路線

a main line to Moscow 前往莫斯科的鐵路幹線

a mainline station 幹線上的車站

branch line (n.) 支線

例句：

Tourists could reach Pingxi District by a branch line named the Pingxi line.

旅客可以搭乘平溪支線到達平溪。

locomotive (n.) 火車頭 (a railway engine)

dining car (n.) 餐車

seat number (n.) 座號

railroad crossing (n.) 平交道

(英式英語為level crossing)

line closure 該線停駛

MP3 088

公車：

bus (n.) 公車

詞彙：

bus driver 公車駕駛

bus fare 公車車資

bus lane 公車專用道

bus route 公車路線

bus stop/station 公車站

night bus 夜間公車

片語：

get on a bus 上公車

get off a bus 下公車

wait for a bus 等公車

catch a bus 追公車

take/ride a bus 坐公車

miss a bus 錯過公車

例句：

If we don't leave soon, we'll miss the last bus.

如果我們不快離開，我們就會錯過末班公車。

The best way to get there is by bus.

到達那裡的最佳方式就是搭公車。

I live on a bus route so I can easily get to work.

我住在公車路線上，所以我上班很方便。

coach (n.) 長途客運、巴士

詞彙：

coach tour/trip/holiday 巴士旅行／巴士假期

a coach trip to Scotland 到蘇格蘭的巴士之旅

例句：

We're going to the airport by coach.

我們要搭客運去機場。

MP3 089

route number 公車路線編號

例句：

When taking a bus, don't just go by the route number, but make sure you get the right direction.

搭公車時，別只顧著看幾號公車，還要確定你坐對方向。

計程車：

taxi/cab (n.) 計程車

詞彙：

taxi rank/taxi stand 計程車招呼站

taxi driver 計程車駕駛

片語：

take a taxi/cab 搭計程車

hail a taxi/cab 招車／叫車

call/order you a taxi 幫你用電話叫車

例句：

I took a taxi from the station to the hotel.

從車站到飯店，我搭計程車。

I tried to hail a taxi but none of them stopped.

我盡力要招計程車，但沒有一台停下來。

It's only a 5 minute taxi ride away.

從那兒到這裡搭計程車大約五分鐘。

meter (n.) 計程車的計費表

例句：

The taxi driver left the meter running while I helped my mum to her front door.

當我扶著我媽進門時，計程車司機繼續跳表計費。

fare (n.) 計程車乘客
(如前所述，車資也是fare)

例句：

A passenger in a cab is a fare.

計程車的乘客也叫作fare。

vacant (adj.) 空的、空車

例句：

In London, the cabs there have a single, simple light: on if vacant, off if occupied.

倫敦的計程車有一個簡單的指示燈，燈亮時表示空車；燈暗時表示已載客(occupied)。

occupied (adj.) 已載客

例句：

It is difficult to hail a taxi on a rainy day because they are often occupied.

下雨天很難招到計程車，因為它們常常都已載客。

MP3 091

汽車：

car (n.) 車子

詞彙：

car crash/accident 車禍

片語：

get in/into a car 上車

get out of a car 下車

例句：

We don't have a car.

我們沒有車。

It's quicker by car.

開車比較快。

You really ought to walk a bit more, rather than taking the car.

你真的應該多走點路，而不是開車。

Diana was killed in a car crash.

Diana在一場車禍中喪生。

Stop the car. I want to get out.

停車！我要下車！

van (n.) 箱型車、商旅車

例句：

We'll have to hire a van to move all this stuff.

我們會需要租一台箱型車來搬運這些東西。

truck (n.) 卡車、聯結車
(英式英語：lorry)

例句：

The road was completely blocked by an overturned truck.

道路因為一台卡車翻覆(overturn)而完全阻塞。

MP3 092

sports car (n.) 跑車

convertible (n.) 敞篷車

limousine (n.) 加長型禮車（簡稱limo）

pickup truck (n.) 小型卡車、小貨卡、載卡多（簡稱pickup或pick-up）

SUV (Sport Utility Vehicle) (n.) 休旅車

trailer (n.) 露營車（英式英語：caravan）

scooter (n.) 速克達、輕型機車

motorcycle (n.) 摩托車

wing mirror (n.) 汽車兩側的後視鏡

rear view mirror (n.) 後視鏡

例句：

Check your rear-view mirror before you drive away.

駕駛前確認你的後視鏡！

horn (n.) 喇叭

例句：

The driver honked her horn.

駕駛按了喇叭。

brake (n.) 剎車

片語：

slam on/hit the brakes 緊急煞車

例句：

The brakes failed and the car crashed into a tree.

剎車失靈了，車子因此撞上一棵樹。

He saw the child run out, so he slammed on the brakes.

他看到孩子衝出來，所以他緊急剎車。

MP3 093

handbrake (n.) 手剎車

例句：

You're supposed to pull up the handbrake whenever you stop on a hill.

每當你將車停在坡道時，你應該要拉手煞車。

manual (adj.) 手動的、手排

詞彙：

a five-speed manual gearbox

五速手排變速器／齒輪箱

automatic (adj.) 自動排檔的

例句：

The car comes with either a manual or an automatic gearbox.

車子通常配有不是手排就是自排的變速箱。

headlight (n.) 頭燈

例句：

It was foggy, and all the cars had their headlights on.

霧很濃，因此所有車子都將大燈打開。

air-conditioning (n.) 空調、冷氣

例句：

I wish my car had an air-conditioning.

但願我的車子有裝冷氣。

engine (n.) 引擎

詞彙：

car engine 汽車引擎

a jet/steam engine 噴射／蒸氣引擎

diesel/petrol engine 柴油／汽油引擎

片語：

stop/turn off/switch off an engine 關掉引擎

start/switch on an engine 發動引擎

例句：

The engine won't start.

引擎發不動。

He switched off the car's engine and waited.

他熄掉引擎，等待。

The battery is flat/dead/gone.

電池沒電了。

My car has got a dead battery.

我車子的電池沒電了。

bumper (n.) 保險桿

詞彙：

bumper sticker 貼在保險桿上的貼紙

front seat (n.) 前座

back seat (n.) 後座

speedometer (n.) 速度錶

windshield/windscreen (n.) 擋風玻璃

windshield wiper/windscreen wiper (n.)
雨刷

steering wheel (n.) 方向盤

air bag (n.) 安全氣囊

accelerator/gas pedal (n.) 油門

gearbox (n.) 齒輪箱

taillight/rear light (n.) 尾燈

brake light (n.) 剎車燈

turn signal (n.) 方向燈
(英式英語：indicator)

license plate/number plate (n.) 車牌

aerial (n.) 天線

petrol tank/fuel tank (n.) 油箱

battery (n.) 電池

MP3 095

drive (v.) 開車、駕駛

詞彙：

driving school 駕訓班

driving test 駕照考試、路試

driving under the influence (DUI)/

driving while intoxicated (DWI) 酒駕

片語：

drive off 駛離

例句：

I drove my daughter to school.

我載我女兒去上學。

I've been driving for 15 years and I've never had an accident.

我開車至今15年，從來沒有肇事過。

Smith was arrested and charged with DUI.

Smith因為酒駕被逮捕和起訴。

I got in the car and drove off.

我上車駛離。

driver's license (n.) 駕照
(英式英語：driving licence)

例句：

Fred lost his driver's license after being caught drunken driving.

Fred因為酒駕被吊銷駕照。

pass (v.) 超車 (英式英語：overtake)

例句：

Always check your rear view mirror before you pass another car.

在超車前一定要檢查後視鏡。

Never try to overtake on a bend.

別在彎道(bend)時超車。

MP3 096

park (v.) 停車

詞彙：

double-park (v.) 並排停車

名詞：

parking (n.) 停車

詞彙：

no parking 禁止停車

parking space/place/spot 停車位

parking lot/car park 停車場

parking meter 計時停車收費表

parking ticket 違規停車的罰單

例句：

Kate parked the car at the side of the road.

Kate將車停在路邊。

I couldn't find a parking space near the restaurant.

我找不到在餐廳附近的停車位。

Free parking is available at the hotel.

旅館提供免費停車。

pull over 路邊停車、或警察攔檢

例句：

Let's pull over and have a look at the map.

我們路邊停一下看看地圖。

The police officer pulled me over because one of my brake lights wasn't working.

警察把我攔下來，因為我其中一個剎車燈壞了。

speed (v.) 超速 (be speeding)

詞彙：

a speeding ticket 超速罰單

例句：

He was caught speeding.

他超速駕駛被逮。

MP3 097

Drivers who are caught speeding risk a heavy fine.

超速的駕駛冒著被高額罰款的風險。

speed limit (n.) 速限

詞彙：

a 50 mph speed limit 速限時速50英哩

片語：

break/go over the speed limit 超速

例句：

Slow down! You're breaking the speed limit.

慢一點！你已經超速了。

traffic (n.) 交通、交通量、交通狀況

詞彙：

rush-hour traffic 尖峰時間的交通

例句：

The traffic noise kept me awake.

交通噪音讓我睡不著。

At that time of night, there was no traffic on the roads.

在夜晚的那個時候，路上已經幾乎沒有車輛。

We were stuck in heavy traffic for more than an hour.

我們困在車陣中超過一小時。

traffic jam/traffic congestion (n.) 塞車

例句：

Roadwork has caused traffic jams throughout the city center.

道路施工導致整個市中心的交通壅塞。

The project aims to reduce traffic congestion.

這個計劃旨在減少交通壅塞。

MP3 098

freeway (n.) 高速公路
(英式英語：motorway)

片語：

get on/enter a freeway 上高速公路

get off/exit a freeway 下高速公路

toll (n.)
過路費、用路費、過橋費、通行費

詞彙：

Electronic Toll Collection (ETC)

高速公路電子收費

例句：

He's got a job collecting tolls at the start of the motorway.

他剛剛找到一個在高速公路起點收費的工作。

exit 出口（英式英語：junction）

例句：

Leave the motorway at Exit 3.

從三號出口下交流道。

street (n.) 街、街道

詞彙：

high street/main street 城鎮中的主要街道

street vendor/musician 攤販／街頭藝人

例句：

I walked on further down the street.

我繼續沿著街道往下走。

Someone just moved in across the street.

對街有人剛搬進來。

Thousands of tourists wander along the streets of Paris.

數以千計的觀光客在巴黎的街道上閒逛 (wander)。

I bought these sunglasses from a street vendor in Florence.

這副太陽眼鏡是我在佛羅倫斯向一個攤販買的。

avenue (n.) 大道、寬敞的路

詞彙：

Fifth Avenue 紐約的第五大道

boulevard (n.) 大馬路、林蔭大道

例句：

We strolled along the boulevard.

我們沿著林蔭大道散步(stroll)。

lane (n.) 巷、車道

詞彙：

fast lane 快車道

slow lane 慢車道

inside lane 內車道

（靠近路肩的車道，台灣的外車道）

outside/passing/overtaking lane 外車道

（超車道，靠近分隔島的車道，台灣的內車道）

bike/cycle lane 單車道

例句：

He drives so fast along those narrow country lanes.

他在窄小的鄉間小徑中高速駕駛。

That man changed lanes without signaling.

那個人沒打方向燈就變換車道。

Use the outside lane for overtaking only.

唯有在超車時才使用外車道。

intersection (n.) 十字路口、交叉路口
(英式英語：junction)

詞彙：

a busy intersection 交通繁忙的路口

例句：

Our school is at the intersection of two main roads.

我們學校就位在兩條幹道的交叉口。

Turn right at the next intersection.

在下個交叉路口右轉。

traffic light (n.) 紅綠燈（多使用複數）

例句：

Turn left at the traffic lights.

在紅綠燈左轉！

When the traffic light turned green, Vivian went ahead.

當號誌轉綠，Vivian便往前進。

speed bump/speed hump (n.) 減速坡

例句：

Local residents are asking for speed bumps to be installed in their street.

當地居民要求在街上設置減速坡。

pedestrian (n.) 行人

詞彙：

pedestrian zones/auto-free zones/car-free zones 行人徒步區

例句：

The death rate for pedestrians hit by cars is unacceptably high.

行人被汽車追撞的致死率高到令人無法接受。

The area is open to cyclists and pedestrians.

這個區域只開放給單車騎士和行人。

pedestrian crossing/crosswalk (n.)

行人穿越道、斑馬線(zebra crossing)

sidewalk (n.) 人行道

(英式英語：pavement)

詞彙：

sidewalk/pavement café

會將桌椅擺上人行道的路邊小館

sidewalk/pavement artist

在人行道上作畫的街頭藝術家

例句：

A small group of journalists waited on the sidewalk outside her house.

一小群記者等在她家外頭的人行道上。

divided highway/dual carriageway (n.)

中間有分隔島區分不同方向來車的公路

one-way traffic (n.) 單行道

hard shoulder (n.) 路肩

traffic circle (n.) 圓環

(英式英語：roundabout)

traffic island (n.) 安全島

traffic sign (n.) 交通號誌

gas station (n.) 加油站

(英式英語：petrol station)

1
0
2

飛機：

airplane (n.) 飛機（簡稱plane）

詞彙：

passenger airplane 客機

片語：

board/get on an airplane 上飛機

get off a plane 下飛機

fly an airplane 飛飛機、開飛機

例句：

After passengers got off the airplane in Vancouver, it continued on its way to New York.

當旅客在溫哥華下機後，該機繼續飛往紐約。

We drove to the airport and caught the next airplane to Nice.

我們開車去機場，然後搭乘下一班飛往尼斯的飛機。

flight (n.) 航班、航線

詞彙：

a long/short flight 長途／短途航線／航班

a domestic flight 國內航線（班）

an international flight 國際航線（班）

a non-stop/direct flight 直飛航線（班）

片語：

book a flight 訂機票

catch a flight 搭飛機

miss a flight 錯過航班

cancel a flight 取消航班

例句：

The flight from New York to Heathrow took about 8 hours.

紐約飛往希斯洛機場的航班需飛行約八小時。

He immediately booked a flight to Mexico City.

他立即訂了飛往墨西哥市的機票。

MP3 103

Have a good flight!

祝你旅途愉快！

take off 起飛

例句：

The plane should take off on time.

飛機應該準時起飛。

land/touch down (v.) 降落

例句：

We expect to be landing in Oslo in about fifty minutes.

我們預期在50分鐘後在奧斯陸的機場降落。

The plane touched down in Sydney at midnight.

飛機抵達雪梨時已是半夜。

airport (n.) 機場

片語：

meet sb/pick sb up at the airport 在機場碰面、接機

arrive at/get to the airport 到達機場

例句：

I checked online and saw that the plane had already touched down at the airport.

我上網查了一下，發現飛機已經在機場降落。

Make sure you get to the airport two hours before your flight.

確保你在飛機起飛的兩小時前到達機場。

One of our representatives will meet you at the airport and take you to your hotel.

我們的代表會在機場跟您碰頭，並且帶您到下榻的旅館。

MP3 104

check-in desk/check-in counter(n.) 報到處

boarding pass/boarding card (n.) 登機証

passport control(n.) 護照檢查處、出境處

例句：

It can take a while to go through passport control in the airport.

在機場通過護照檢查處可能會花一點時間。

security (n.) 安檢處

duty-free shop (n.) 免稅商店

landing card (n.) 入境卡

baggage reclaim (n.) 行李提領處

customs (n.) 海關

runway (n.) 跑道

例句：

The plane takes off from the runway.

飛機從跑到起飛。

gate (n.) 閘口、登機門

例句：

All passengers for flight LH122 please proceed to gate 19.

航班編號LH122的旅客請前往19號閘口。

pilot (n.) 飛機駕駛

例句：

Chesley Sulenberger is the pilot who safely landed a plane in the Hudson River in 2009.

Chesley Sulenberger是2009年成功將飛機迫降紐約哈德森河的飛機駕駛。

He always wanted to be an airline pilot.

他之前一直想成為民航機駕駛。

MP3 105

seat belt (n.) 安全帶

例句：

Please fasten your seat belt.

請繫上安全帶。

flight attendant (n.) 空服員

aisle seat (n.) 走道位

middle seat (n.) 中間位

window seat (n.) 靠窗位

overhead compartment/
overhead locker (n.) 上層置物箱（櫃）

window blind/window shade (n.)
遮光板

blanket (n.) 毛毯

headphones (n.) 耳機

tray (n.) 機上的餐桌

in-flight (adj./adv.) 航程中的

詞彙：

in-flight entertainment/meal/movie

航程中提供給旅客的娛樂／餐飲／電影

in-flight security 空中保安、航程中的安全

例句：

Passengers are not allowed to use their cell phones in-flight.

旅客在飛行途中禁止使用手機。

turbulence (n.) 亂流

例句：

We might be experiencing some turbulence on this flight due to an approaching electrical storm.

我們搭乘的航班很可能會遇到亂流，因為我們正逼近一個挾帶著雷電的暴風雨圈。

MP3 106

short-haul flight (n.) 短程飛行

詞彙：

a short-haul flight within the UK

英國境內的短程飛行

long-haul flight (n.) 長途飛行

例句：

It is a long-haul flight from London to Hong Kong.

從倫敦飛香港是段長途飛行。

jet lag (n.) 時差

形容詞：

jet-lagged (adj.)

例句：

I'm suffering from jet lag but I'll feel better after a good night's sleep.

我深受時差之苦，但我想經過一夜好眠我就會好很多。

James is a bit jet-lagged after a long-haul flight from Taiwan to New York.

從台灣飛往紐約之後，James有一點時差。

MP3 107

船：

boat (n.) (小)船

詞彙：

fishing boat 漁船

motorboat 汽艇、快艇

例句：

Are you travelling by boat or by air?

你要搭船還是搭飛機？

We took turns to row the boat up the river.

我們輪流划船，逆流而上。

ship (n.) 船艦、大船

詞彙：

cargo ship 貨船

supply ship 補給艦

naval ship/battleship 戰艦、軍艦

merchant ship 商船

sailing ship 帆船

例句：

There were over 350 passengers aboard the ship.

一共三百五十幾位乘客登船。

ferry (n.) 渡船

片語：

take/catch the ferry 搭乘渡輪

例句：

There is no ferry service to the island in the winter.

冬天時渡輪不提供載客服務。

He went by overnight ferry from Dover to Calais.

他從多佛(英國城市)搭乘在海上過夜的渡輪前往加萊(法國城市)。

MP3 108

cruise ship/cruise liner (n.) 豪華郵輪

例句：

RMS Titanic was probably the most famous cruise liner in history.

鐵達尼號可能是歷史上最有名的豪華郵輪。

canoe (n.) 獨木舟

動詞：

canoe (v.) 划獨木舟

例句：

They died in a canoeing accident.

他們在一場獨木舟意外中過世。

submarine (n.) 潛水艇

詞彙：

nuclear submarine 核子潛艇

submarine base 潛艇基地

submarine sandwich 潛艇堡
（長條形的三明治）

yacht (n.)遊艇

port (n.) 港

詞彙：

naval port 軍港

fishing port 漁港

例句：

We had a good view of all the ships coming into the port.

我們有很棒的視野可以看到所有進港的船隻。

We'll have to spend 10 days in port for repairs.

我們將留港十天修理船隻。

MP3 109

harbor (n.) 港灣
(英式拼音：harbour)

詞彙：

Pearl Harbor 珍珠港

例句：

The wind kept us in harbor until the following afternoon.

強風將我們困在港口到隔天下午。

Our hotel room overlooked a pretty little fishing harbor.

我們的旅館鳥瞰一個美麗的小漁港。

sail (v.) 航行、啟航

名詞：

sail (n.) 船帆、航行

The ship was sailing to China.

那艘船開往中國。

The boat sailed along the coast.

那艘船沿著海岸線行駛。

Their ship sails for Bombay next Friday.

他們的船下週五即將啟航前往孟買。

It is a two-day sail from here to the nearest island.

從這兒到最近的離島要兩天的航程。

sailor (n.) 水手

例句：

We are all experienced sailors.

我們都是老經驗的水手。

seasick (adj.) 暈船的

例句：

I felt seasick, so I went up on deck for some fresh air.

因為有點暈船，所以我上甲板來呼吸新鮮空氣。

deck (n.) 艙面、甲板

詞彙：

upper/lower deck 上層／下層甲板

例句：

We sat on deck until it was dark.

我們坐在甲板上直到天黑。

The first-class cabins were on the upper deck.

頭等艙房位在上層甲板。

bridge (n.) 艦橋

cabin (n.) 客艙

lifeboat (n.) 救生艇

life jacket (n.) 救生衣

衣服

Clothing

MP3 111

clothes (n.) 衣服

詞彙：

school/sport clothes 制服／運動服

maternity clothes 孕婦裝

clothes basket 洗衣籃

clothes shop 服裝店

designer clothes 知名設計師設計的服裝

片語：

put on/take off clothes 穿上／脫掉衣服

例句：

She usually wears designer clothes.

她通常都穿知名設計師設計的服裝。

Why don't you take those wet clothes off?

你怎麼不脫掉那身濕衣服？

She looks odd in those clothes.

她穿那樣看起來很奇怪。

outfit (n.)
一整套衣服、(一整套)外觀、裝扮

詞彙：

a cowboy outfit 牛仔裝

例句：

She bought a new outfit for the wedding party.

她為了婚禮購置了一整套新衣服。

sleeve (n.) 袖子

詞彙：

short/long sleeves 短袖／長袖

例句：

Vivian was wearing a dress with short sleeves.

Vivian穿一件短袖洋裝。

You'd better roll your sleeves up or you'll get them dirty.

你最好將袖子捲起來，否則它們會被弄髒。

MP3 112

collar (n.) 領子

例句：

He had his collar turned up against the cold.

他將領子豎起來以抵擋寒冷。

He was so angry so he grabbed me by the collar.

因為太生氣了，所以他揪住我的領口。

He loosened his collar and tie.

他鬆開他的領口和領帶(tie)。

pocket (n.) 口袋

片語：

put something into a pocket 把東西放進口袋

take something from/out of a pocket

把東西從口袋掏出來

turn out/empty your pocket 清空口袋

例句：

She took some coins out of her pocket.

她從口袋裡掏出一些零錢。

The police officer asked them to empty their pockets.

警察命令他們將口袋清空。

He slipped his wallet into an inside pocket of his jacket.

他將皮夾(wallet)塞入他外套(jacket)的內袋。

zipper (n.) 拉鏈（英式英語：zip）

片語：

do up/undo a zipper 拉上／解開拉鏈

例句：

I can't open my bag. The zipper is stuck.

我沒辦法打開我的包包。拉鏈卡住了。

Your zip's undone at the back.

你背後的拉鏈鬆開了。

MP3 113

button (n.) 扣子

片語：

do up/undo (fasten/unfasten) the buttons

扣上／解開鈕扣

例句：

After a long meeting, John undid the top button of his shirt.

在冗長的會議後，John解開襯衫的第一顆鈕扣。

suit (n.) 西裝／套裝（女生為裙裝）

例句：

Chris wore a suit and tie to the wedding.

Chris 穿西裝打領帶去參加婚禮。

She wore a dark blue suit.

她穿一件深藍色的套裝。

pantsuit (n.) 女生穿的褲子式套裝
(英式英語：trouser suit)

例句：

Lisa bought a very smart pantsuit for her job interviews.

Lisa為了工作面試買了一套很棒的褲式套裝。

jacket (n.) 外套、夾克

詞彙：

suit jacket 西裝外套

a tweed/linen/denim/leather jacket

一件粗花呢／亞麻／丹寧(牛仔)／皮夾克

例句：

The keys are in my jacket pocket.

鑰匙在我的外套口袋。

He looks good in jeans and a leather jacket.

他穿牛仔褲配皮夾克時看起來很帥。

MP3 114

blazer (n.) 獵裝、或者西裝式的制服外套(比正式的西裝外套休閒)

coat (n.) 外套、大衣

詞彙：

overcoat 長大衣

raincoat 雨衣

trench coat 綁帶的長風／雨衣

a fur coat 毛皮大衣

例句：

The lab assistants wear long white coats.

實驗室的助理罩著白色的長外衣。

Put your coat on.

穿上你的大衣！

windbreaker (n.) 風衣

cape (n.) 披肩、斗篷

sweater (n.) 套頭毛衣
(英式英語：jumper)

詞彙：

a V-necked sweater V領毛衣

a red wooly jumper 一件紅色羊毛衫

例句：

Put a sweater on if you're cold.

如果你覺得冷，就套上毛衣。

cardigan (n.)
開襟毛衣、開襟的針織上衣

例句：

We found a gray cardigan with a hole in the right elbow.

我們找到一件灰色的開襟針織衫。它的左手肘處破了一個洞。

MP3 115

sweatshirt (n.) 厚運動衫

例句：

Bill was dressed casually in jeans and a sweatshirt.

Bill隨性地穿著牛仔褲(jeans)搭配厚運動衫。

hoodie (n.) 帽T

例句：

The suspect was last seen wearing a dark hoodie and armed with a gun.

嫌犯最後被目擊時穿著一件暗色帽T並且持有一把手槍。

vest (n.) 西裝背心、男用馬甲 (英式英語：waistcoat)

詞彙：

a tactical/bulletproof vest 戰術／防彈背心

shirt (n.) 襯衫

詞彙：

a cotton/silk/denim shirt

一件棉質／絲質／牛仔(丹寧) 襯衫

a short-/long-sleeved shirt

一件短袖／長袖襯衫

a striped/white shirt 一件條紋／白襯衫

例句：

I have to wear a shirt and tie to work.

我得穿襯衫打領帶(tie)去上班。

One of his shirt buttons was missing.

他的襯衫掉了一個鈕扣 (button)。

blouse (n.) 婦女穿的襯衫或罩衫

詞彙：

a cotton/silk/nylon blouse

一件棉質／絲質／尼龍襯衫

例句：

Do you like my new blouse?

你喜歡我的新襯衫嗎？

dress (n.) 洋裝

詞彙：

a long/short dress 長／短洋裝

a wedding dress 婚紗

a pink cotton dress 一件粉紅棉質洋裝

例句：

I'd never seen her in a dress before.

我從沒看過她穿洋裝。

Mary wore a long red dress.

Mary穿一件紅色的長洋裝。

polo shirt (n.) 馬球衫、polo衫

T-shirt (n.)T恤

tank top (n.) 坦克背心

bottoms (n.) 下半身部位的衣物

詞彙：

pajama bottoms (n.) 睡褲

例句：

I usually just wear jogging bottoms and a T-shirt.

我通常只穿運動褲和T恤。

Have you seen my pajama bottoms anywhere?

你有看到我的睡褲嗎？

pants (n.) 褲子（英式英語：trousers）

詞彙：

a pair of pants 一條褲子

cargo pants/cargo trousers

工作褲（口袋很多的褲子）

MP3 117

sweatpants 運動長褲

例句：

Mary was wearing dark blue pants and a white sweater.

Mary穿一件深藍色的褲子搭配白毛衣。

I need a new pair of trousers to go with the jacket.

我需要一件新褲子來搭配這件外套。

jeans (n.) 牛仔褲

詞彙：

a pair of jeans 一條牛仔褲

jeans and T-shirt T恤牛仔褲

skinny 激瘦／緊身／窄管

slim 小直筒

straight 直筒

bootcut 喇叭

例句：

He never wears jeans for work.

他不曾穿牛仔褲去上班。

shorts (n.) 短褲、內褲

詞彙：

a pair of shorts 一條短褲

Bermuda shorts 百慕達褲

cargo shorts 多口袋的工作短褲

cycling shorts 單車短褲

（騎乘單車時穿著的緊身短褲）

tourists in shorts and T-shirts

穿著短褲T恤的觀光客

例句：

She put on a pair of shorts and a T-shirt.

她套上一條短褲和T恤。

skirt (n.) 裙子

詞彙：

a long/short skirt 一件長／短裙

a leather/cotton skirt 皮裙／棉裙

a pencil skirt/pleated skirt 直裙／百褶裙

例句：

She was wearing a short skirt and a blouse.

她穿著一件短裙和罩衫。

leggings (n.) 緊身褲、內搭褲

詞彙：

a pair of leggings 一條緊身內搭褲

wetsuit/wet suit (n.) 潛水衣、防寒衣

詞彙：

divers in wetsuits 穿著防寒衣的潛水伕

bikini (n.) 比基尼

詞彙：

a bikini top 比基尼的上半部

bikini bottoms 比基尼的下半部

例句：

I've found my bikini bottoms but not my top.

我找到我比基尼的下半部但不是上半身。

One-piece swimsuits are more fashionable than bikinis this year.

今年連身泳裝(one-piece)要比比基尼更為時尚。

chinos (n.) 棉褲（例如卡其褲）

miniskirt (n.) 迷你裙

sarong (n.) 沙龍

swimsuit/swimwear(n.) 泳裝

swim shorts (n.) 泳褲 (英式英語：swimming trunks)

MP3 119

貼身衣物

pajamas (n.) 睡衣
(英式英語：pyjamas)

詞彙：

striped pajamas 條紋睡衣

pajama party 睡衣派對（在此pajama不加s）

例句：

It was ten o'clock in the morning but he was still in his pajamas.

早上十點了，但他還穿著他的睡衣。

slip (n.) 女用襯裙

詞彙：

a white silk slip 一件白色絲質襯裙

underwear (n.) 內衣褲

詞彙：

thermal underwear 發熱衣

例句：

He was standing there in his underwear.

他僅著內衣褲站在那兒。

You just need to take a change of underwear.

你只需要帶一套換洗內衣褲。

lingerie (n.) 女用內衣褲

例句：

Nancy wanted to buy some lingerie on her way home.

Nancy想在回家途中買幾件內衣褲。

bra (n.) 胸罩

詞彙：

MP3 120

sports bra 運動內衣

underpants (n.) 內褲

(英式英語：pants)

詞彙：

a pair of underpants 一條內褲

boxer briefs (n.) 合身的四角內褲

boxer shorts (n.) 寬鬆的四角內褲

briefs (n.) 三角內褲

panties (n.) 女用三角內褲

(英式英語：knickers)

thong (n.) 丁字褲

bathrobe/dressing gown (n.)

晨袍、浴袍、在家穿的袍子

tights (n.) 褲襪、絲襪、緊身襪

sock (n.) 襪子

詞彙：

a pair of socks 一雙襪子

nylon/woolen/cotton socks

尼龍襪／羊毛襪／棉襪

ankle/knee socks 踝襪／及膝襪

例句：

The little girl was wearing mismatched socks.

那個小女生穿錯襪子了。(穿了一雙不同花色的襪子)

shoe (n.) 鞋子

詞彙：

walking/running shoes 走路鞋／跑鞋

shoe polish 鞋油

shoe shop 鞋店

片語：

in someone's shoes 設身處地、在某人所處的情境下

MP3 121

例句：

Mark bought several pairs of shoes.

Mark買了幾雙鞋。

What would you do if you were in my shoes?

如果你身在我目前的處境，你會怎麼做？

shoelace(n.) 鞋帶

片語：

tie/untie; do/undo shoelaces綁／鬆綁鞋帶

例句：

Your shoelaces are undone.

你的鞋帶鬆了。

Do/Tie up your shoelaces, Paul.

Paul, 把鞋帶綁好。

sandal (n.) 涼鞋

例句：

Many people wear sandals in the summer.

許多人在夏天穿涼鞋。

slipper (n.) 室內拖鞋

例句：

After a hard day's work, John loved relaxing in his slippers.

一天辛勞的工作後，John喜歡穿著拖鞋放鬆。

boot (n.) 靴子

詞彙：

ankle/knee/thigh boots

高度到腳踝／膝蓋／大腿的靴子

walking/hiking/riding/football boots

走路靴／健行靴／馬靴／足球鞋

例句：

MP3 122

She wore black leather ankle boots.

她穿一雙黑色款的皮踝靴。

rain boot/rubber boot (n.) 雨鞋

(英式英語：wellington/welly)

(英式英語：wellingtons/wellies)

例句：

He left his muddy wellingtons outside the back door.

他將滿是泥濘的雨鞋放在後門外。

sneaker (n.) 運動鞋

(英式英語為trainer)

詞彙：

a pair of white sneakers 一雙白球鞋

thongs/flip-flops (n.) 人字拖

slip-ons/loafers (n.) 休閒鞋／樂福鞋

(一種低跟、無鞋帶，容易穿脫的鞋，

可輕鬆可正式)

boat shoes/deck shoes (n.) 帆船鞋

spike (n.) 釘鞋

high heels (n.) 高跟鞋

MP3 123

配飾

hat (n.) 帽子

詞彙：

straw hat 草帽

sun hat 遮陽帽

top hat 紳士帽、高帽

trucker hat 卡車司機帽

hard hat 工地帽(通常是黃色的那種帽子)

例句：

Maria was wearing a gorgeous new hat.

Maria戴著一頂美麗的新帽子。

cap (n.) 帽子、制服帽

詞彙：

a nurse's/chauffeur's/sailor's cap

護士帽／司機帽／水手帽

a swimming/bathing/shower cap 泳帽／浴帽

baseball cap (n.) 棒球帽

peaked cap (n.) 大盤帽（軍人、警察、駕駛）

helmet (n.) 安全帽

詞彙：

a cycle helmet 單車安全帽

a motorcycle helmet 機車安全帽

beret (n.) 貝雷帽

barrette/hair clip (n.) 髮夾
（英式英語：hair slide）

headband (n.) 頭帶、髮箍、髮帶

MP3 124

scarf (n.) 圍巾

複數：

scarves

詞彙：

a knitted/woolen/silk scarf

一條針織的／羊毛的／絲質的圍巾

glove (n.) 手套

詞彙：

a pair of gloves 一副手套

leather/woolen/rubber gloves

毛皮／羊毛／橡膠手套

handkerchief (n.) 手帕

例句：

She took out her handkerchief and blew her nose loudly.

她拿出她的手帕並且大聲地擤鼻子。

jewelry (n.) 珠寶

(英式英語：jewellery)

詞彙：

jewelry box 珠寶盒

a piece of jewelry 一件珠寶

例句：

She wears a lot of gold jewelry.

她穿戴許多金飾。

She's got some lovely pieces of jewelry.

她有一些很精美的珠寶。

pin (n.) 別針／胸針／別針類的飾品

(英式英語：brooch)

例句：

MP3 125

There are several ways to wear pins.

穿戴別針類的飾品有幾種方式。

She wore a small silver brooch.

她別了一個小小的銀製胸針。

necklace (n.) 項鍊

詞彙：

a gold/silver/pearl/coral necklace

一條金／銀／珍珠／珊瑚項鍊

例句：

She was wearing a necklace of glass beads.

她戴了一條玻璃珠串成的項鍊。

watch (n.) 手錶

片語：

look at/glance at/consult one's watch

看／瞄一眼／錶

例句：

My watch has stopped.

我的錶停了。

He glanced nervously at his watch.

他緊張地瞄了一眼他的手錶。

bangle/bracelet (n.) 手環、手鐲

詞彙：

a gold/silver/diamond bracelet

一只金／銀／鑽石手鐲

ring (n.) 戒指

詞彙：

a diamond ring 鑽戒

例句：

He bought her a diamond ring.

他為她買了一只鑽戒。

MP3 126

She had a ring on every finger.

她每隻手指上都有戒指。

earring (n.) 耳環

詞彙：

a pair of earrings 一對耳環

gold/diamond/pearl earrings

金／鑽石／珍珠耳環

例句：

She was wearing a pair of beautiful pearl earrings.

她戴一對美麗的珍珠耳環。

He was wearing an earing in his left ear.

他在左耳戴上一隻耳環。

glasses (n.) 眼鏡

詞彙：

a pair of glasses 一副眼鏡

reading glasses 老花眼鏡

例句：

Nowadays, most children wear glasses.

現在的孩子多半都戴眼鏡。

Steve put on his reading glasses.

Steve戴上他的老花眼鏡。

sunglasses (n.) 太陽眼鏡

詞彙：

a pair of sunglasses 一副太陽眼鏡

contact lens (n.) 隱形眼鏡

例句：

I usually wear contact lenses, but I sometimes wear glasses when my eyes are tired.

我通常會戴隱形眼鏡，但當眼睛疲勞時，我會戴眼鏡。

MP3 127

belt (n.) 腰帶

詞彙：

leather belt 皮帶

片語：

put on/fasten a belt 繫皮帶

do/undo, buckle/unbuckle one's belt

繫緊／鬆開皮帶

例句：

She fastened her belt tightly around her waist.

她將腰帶緊緊地繫在腰上。

James had eaten so much that he had to unbuckle his belt.

James因為吃太飽，所以鬆開了他的皮帶。

necktie/tie (n.) 領帶

詞彙：

tie pin 領帶夾

例句：

His tie was held in place with a small diamond pin.

一枚小小的鑽石別針固定著他的領帶。

For work, you should wear a collar and tie.

工作時，你應該穿襯衫打領帶。（collar是領子的意思，在此句中延伸為襯衫）

White tie (or full dress) is the most formal evening dress code in Western fashion.

在西方社會中，white tie是最正式的晚宴穿著規定。

bow tie (n.) 領結

cufflink (n.) 袖扣

key ring (n.) 鑰匙圈

cigarette case/box/tin (n.) 菸盒

MP3 128

dress code (n.) 服裝規定

例句：

My school had a very strict dress code.

我的學校有嚴格的服裝規定。

There were plans to introduce a dress code for civil servants.

有些計劃將引進公務員的服裝規定。

casual 隨意穿著，最典型的就是T恤牛仔褲。

business casual

男生穿有領子有袖子的上衣，

像是襯衫或polo衫，不打領帶。

女生穿洋裝。

smart casual

男生穿有領子有袖子的上衣，

像是襯衫或polo衫，領帶可打可不打。

女生穿洋裝。

informal/business/suit and necktie

正式服裝，男生穿西裝，

女生穿套裝或禮服。

semi-formal/black tie/tuxedo

男生通常要穿三件式黑西裝、白襯衫、

打黑領結。女生穿晚禮服。

formal wear/formal dress/white tie

最正式。男生要穿白背心，打白領結。

女生穿正式晚禮服。

MP3 129

包包

suitcase (n.) 行李箱

例句：

Have you packed your suitcase yet?

你打包行李了嗎？

purse (n.) 女用手提包、小錢包 (英式英語：handbag)

詞彙：

change/coin purse 零錢包

leather purse 真皮小包

例句：

She finally found her keys in her purse.

她最終在她的手提包裡找到鑰匙。

Julie opened her backpack and took out her purse.

Julie打開她的背包並且拿出小錢包。

wallet (n.) 皮夾（英式英語：purse）

例句：

I've only got 10 dollars in my wallet.

我的皮夾裡只有10塊錢。

John took a credit card out of his wallet.

John從皮夾裡掏出一張信用卡。

backpack (n.) 背包

briefcase (n.) 公事包

messenger bag (n.) 側背包

只要會這些就夠 英文單字

ESSENTIAL WORDS FOR EVERYDAY USE

住

Accomodation

apartment (n.) 公寓
(英式英語：flat)

例句：

I'll give you the keys to my apartment.

我會給你我公寓的鑰匙。

Let's meet at my flat.

大家在我的公寓碰面吧！

house (n.) 房子

片語：

to buy/rent a house　買／租房子

例句：

John lives in a little house.

John住在一個小房子裡。

Why don't you come over to our house for coffee?

你們要不要來我們家喝咖啡？

cottage (n.) 農舍、小屋

例句：

My uncle lived in a small cottage by the river.

我的叔叔住在河畔的小屋裡。

townhouse/townhome (n.) 連棟住宅 (英式英語：terrace)

floor (n.) 樓層、地板

詞彙：

a wooden floor 木質地板

例句：

Our classroom is on the second floor.

我們的教室在二樓。

We are now on the top floor of the apartment.

我們現在正在這幢公寓的頂樓。

MP3 131

The restaurant floor needs cleaning.

這餐廳的地板需要清理。

We were sitting on the floor watching TV.

我們坐在地上看電視。

stairs (n.) 樓梯

片語：

go up/down the stairs 上、下樓梯

例句：

I heard footsteps on the stairs.

我聽到樓梯上有腳步聲。

Go up the stairs and the classroom is on the left.

上樓梯後教室就在左手邊。

elevator (n.) 電梯（英式英語：lift）

例句：

Do you want to take the elevator or use the stairs?

你想坐電梯還是走樓梯？

Take the lift to the sixth floor.

搭電梯到六樓。

escalator (n.) 手扶梯

例句：

The new department store has escalators to carry customers from one floor to another.

這間新的百貨公司有手扶梯方便顧客上下樓。

passage/corridor (n.) 走廊

例句：

Maggie's office is at the end of the corridor.

Maggie的辦公室在走道的盡頭。

The bathroom is on the right at the end of the passage.

廁所(bathroom)在走道盡頭的右手邊。

wall (n.) 牆壁

詞彙：

walls have ears 隔牆有耳

例句：

The walls in this apartment are so thin that you can hear about every word the neighbors say.

這公寓的牆薄到你可以聽見鄰居說的每一個字。

Michael leans against the wall.

Michael靠在牆上。

ceiling (n.) 天花板

詞彙：

rooms with high ceilings 挑高的房間

glass ceiling 玻璃天花板

（指女性在職場上遇到的升遷障礙）

roof (n.) 屋頂

例句：

The roof is leaking again.

屋頂又漏水了。

They finally found the cat up on the roof.

他們最終在屋頂上找到那隻貓。

attic/loft (n.) 閣樓

例句：

I've put all the baby equipment up in the loft.

我把所有嬰兒用品堆放到閣樓。

John's got boxes of old clothes in the attic.

John把幾箱舊衣服放在閣樓。

basement (n.) 地下室

例句：

I stored my books in the basement.

我把我的書存放在地下室。

balcony (n.) 陽台、露臺

例句：

After dinner, we had drinks on the hotel balcony.

晚餐後，我們在酒店的露臺上喝飲料。

drive/driveway (n.) 車道

例句：

I parked in the driveway.

我把車停在車道上。

There is a BMW in the drive.

車道上有一輛BMW。

garage (n.) 車庫

例句：

Did you put your car in the garage?

你把車停到車庫了嗎？

yard/garden (n.) 花園、庭院

詞彙：

front/back yard/garden 前／後院

roof garden 空中花園

beer garden 酒吧的室外區

例句：

Mary raises chickens in the yard.

Mary在院子裡養雞。

The children are playing in the back garden.

孩子們在後院嬉戲。

MP3 134

lawn (n.) 草皮

片語：

mow/cut the lawn 修剪／割草皮

例句：

Let's have a picnic on the lawn.

我們在草皮上野餐吧！

Will you mow the lawn at the weekend?

你週末會除草嗎？

greenhouse (n.) 溫室

詞彙：

the greenhouse effect 温室效應

例句：

Nicole grows a lot of tomatoes in her greenhouse.

Nicole在她的溫室裡種滿蕃茄。

weed (n.) 雜草

詞彙：

weedkiller/weed-killer 除草劑

例句：

My garden was overgrown with weeds.

我的庭院裡雜草密佈。

A chemical weedkiller can be used to kill persistent weeds.

有一種化學除草劑可用來去除生命力旺盛的雜草。

hedge (n.) 樹籬

片語：

trim the hedge 修剪樹籬

例句：

We crawled through a gap in the hedge.

我們匍匐穿過樹籬間的一個縫隙。

lawn mower (n.) 除草機

watering can (n.) 澆水器

flower bed (n.) 花圃

fence (n.) 柵欄、籬笆

door (n.) 門

詞彙：

the front/back/side door 前／後／側門

a sliding door 滑動的門

片語：

knock on the door 敲門

open the door 開門

close/shut the door 關門

slam the door 甩門

lock the door 鎖門

answer the door 應門（當有人敲門或按門鈴時）

例句：

The door to his room was locked.

他房間的門是鎖著的。

Jack ran out, slamming the door behind him.

Jack衝出去後甩上門！

The people next door aren't very friendly.

隔壁鄰居並不友善。

threshold (n.) 門檻

例句：

He opened the door and stepped across the threshold.

他打開門並且跨過門檻。

doorbell (n.) 門鈴

片語：

ring the doorbell 按門鈴

MP3 136

doorknob (n.) 門把

doorstop (n.) 門擋

mail slot/letterbox (n.) 信箱

light (n.) 燈

片語：

turn/switch/put on a light 開燈

turn/switch/put off a light 熄燈

例句：

We're having a mixture of wall lights and ceiling lights in different parts of the house.

我們在房子四周混搭了各式各樣的壁燈和天花板燈。

I turned on the light in the bedroom.

我將寢室的燈打開。

Don't forget to switch off the lights when you go out.

出門前別忘了關燈。

heater (n.) 暖氣

fan/gas/electric heater

風扇式／瓦斯／電暖氣

例句：

Did you turn off the heater?

你關暖氣了嗎？

furniture (n.) 傢俱

詞彙：

office furniture 辦公用的傢俱

garden furniture 庭院用的傢俱

例句：

The only piece of furniture I have in my office is a desk.

我辦公室裡唯一的傢俱就是一張書桌。

MP3 137

John helped me choose the furniture for my house.

John協助我挑選我家的傢俱。

appliance (n.) 家電用品

例句:

Things like vacuum cleaners, washing machines and televisions are household appliances.

吸塵器、洗衣機和電視都是家電用品。

浴廁：

bathroom (n.) 廁所、浴廁

例句：

Where is the bathroom?

請問廁所在哪？

I would like to go to the bathroom.

我想上廁所。

bath (n.) 沐浴、洗澡

片語：

take/have a bath 洗澡

例句：

I'll have a bath and go to bed.

我要去洗澡然後上床睡覺。

How often do you take a bath?

你多久洗澡一次？

toilet (n.) 馬桶、廁所

詞彙：

public toilets 公共廁所

toilet seat 馬桶座

toilet paper 衛生紙

toilet roll 捲筒式衛生紙

toilet brush 馬桶刷

片語：

flush the toilet 沖馬桶

例句：

Can I use your toilet?

我可以借用你的廁所嗎？

Always wash your hands after you go to the toilet.

上完廁所後要洗手。

He flushed the toilet.

他沖馬桶。

I was using the toilet when the phone rang.

電話鈴響時，我正在上廁所。

tissue (n.) 面紙

詞彙：

bathroom/toilet tissue 衛生紙

例句：

She handed me a tissue just as I sneezed.

當我打噴嚏時，她遞給我一張面紙。

He used a piece of tissue to clean his glasses.

他用一張面紙擦眼鏡。

razor (n.) 刮鬍刀

詞彙：

MP3 139

electric razor 電動刮鬍刀

disposable razor 用過即丟的簡易刮鬍刀

shave (v.) 刮、剃掉毛髮

詞彙：

shaving cream/shaving foam 刮鬚泡沫

片語：

shave one's head/legs/armpits 剃頭髮／腳毛／腋毛

例句：

He hadn't shaved for days.

他幾天沒刮鬍子了。

When my dad shaved his beard off, he looked ten years younger.

當我爸爸剃掉他的鬍子時，他看起來年輕了十歲。

comb (n.) 梳子、梳理頭髮

動詞：

comb (v.) 梳頭髮、整理頭髮

例句：

Your hair needs a good comb.

你的頭髮需要好好梳理一番。

I don't even have time to comb my hair.

我甚至沒有時間梳理頭髮。

towel (n.) 毛巾

詞彙：

bath towel 浴巾

towel rail 毛巾桿、毛巾架

towel holder 毛巾架

paper towel 紙巾

tea/kitchen towel 餐巾紙

例句：

Lucy wrapped herself in a towel after her shower.

Lucy沐浴後將自己用浴巾圍起來。

The school provides the children with paper towels to dry their hands.

學校提供紙巾給孩子擦手。

mirror (n.) 鏡子

例句：

She was looking at her reflection in the mirror.

她注視著自己在鏡中的倒影(reflection)。

shampoo (n.) 洗髮精 、洗頭髮

詞彙：

a bottle of shampoo 一瓶洗髮精

動詞：

shampoo (v.) 用洗髮精洗頭髮

例句：

What kind of shampoo do you use?

你用什麼洗髮精？

Peggy went to the salon for a shampoo and set.

Peggy去美容院(salon)洗頭髮和做造型。

Steve shampooed my hair and then Duncan cut it.

Steve幫我洗頭，然後Duncan幫我剪頭髮。

conditioner (n.) 護髮乳

詞彙：

fabric conditioner (softener) 衣物柔軟精

bathtub (n.) 浴缸（英式英語：bath）

flush toilet (n.) 抽水馬桶

flush handle (n.) 沖水桿

air freshener (n.) 空氣芳香劑

soap (n.) 肥皂

body wash/shower gel (n.) 沐浴乳

MP3 141

facial wash (n.) 洗面乳

hand wash (n.) 洗手乳

hairdryer/hairdrier (n.) 吹風機

shower (n.) 淋浴間、蓮蓬頭

詞彙：

shower head 蓮蓬頭

shower cap 浴帽

shower curtain 浴簾

例句：

The shower is broken. You'll have to have a bath.

蓮蓬頭壞掉了，你得改用盆浴。

Why does the phone always ring when I'm in the shower?

為什麼電話總是當我在淋浴時響起？

drain (n.) 出水孔

例句：

The flood was caused by a blocked drain.

阻塞的排水孔造成這次淹水。

She accidently dropped her ring down a drain in the road.

她不小心將她的戒指掉到路上的排水孔裡。

trash can (n.) 垃圾桶 (英式英語：bin)

例句：

Do you want this or shall I throw it in the trash can?

這你還要嗎？還是我把它丟進垃圾桶？

sponge (n.) 沐浴球、海綿

tile (n.) 磁磚

MP3 142

sanitary napkin/sanitary pad/pad (n.)
衛生棉

toothbrush (n.) 牙刷

toothpaste (n.) 牙膏

floss (n.) 牙線

mouthwash (n.) 漱口水

make-up remover (n.) 卸妝棉

lotion (n.) 乳液

body lotion (n.) 身體乳液

臥房

bedroom (n.) 臥房

詞彙：

the master bedroom 主臥房

a spare bedroom 客房

a two-bedroom apartment 一個兩房的公寓

a hotel with 50 bedrooms

一個50間客房的旅館

例句：

You can stay in the spare bedroom.

你可以睡客房。

wardrobe (n.)

衣櫥、也引申為某人所擁有的衣物

詞彙：

summer/winter wardrobe

(某人所有的)夏季/冬季衣物

例句：

Jane is showing me her wardrobe.

Jane正向我展示她的衣櫥。

Can you hang these in the wardrobe, please?

可否麻煩你幫我將這些衣服吊到衣櫃裡？

I sometimes feel that my summer wardrobe is rather lacking.

我沒有太多夏天的衣服。

closet (n.) 衣櫃

詞彙：

a closet full of beautiful clothes

一個裝滿漂亮衣服的衣櫃

片語：

come out of the closet (come out)

出櫃（同志公開自己的性向）

shelf (n.) 櫃子中的隔層、夾層

複數：

shelves

詞彙：

top/bottom shelf 最上層／最下層

例句：

Put it back on the top shelf.

將它放回櫃子裡的最上層。

The sweaters are on the bottom shelf.

毛衣都放在最下層。

dresser (n.) 抽屜式衣櫃（五斗櫃）

例句：

MP3 144

This eight-drawer dresser will be a welcome addition to any bedroom.

這一個八個抽屜(drawer)的衣櫃會是為每個房間加分的傢俱。

drawer (n.) 抽屜

詞彙：

right-hand/left-hand drawer

右手邊／左手邊的抽屜

例句：

I keep my socks in the bottom drawer.

我將襪子收在底層抽屜。

The photos are in the top drawer of my desk.

照片在我書桌的最上層抽屜裡。

hanger (n.) 衣架

例句：

She took off her coat and hung it on a hanger.

她脫掉大衣並且將它吊在衣架上。

bed (n.) 床

詞彙：

double bed/single bed 雙人床／單人床

air bed 充氣床

sofa bed 沙發床

bunk bed 上下鋪

camp bed 行軍床

four poster bed 四腳有床柱的床

片語：

go to bed 上床睡覺

get out of bed 起床、下床

make the bed 整理床(包含摺被子、拉平床單等等)

例句：

MP3 145

There are two single beds in the hotel room.

旅館房間裡有兩張單人床。

When did you go to bed last night?

你昨晚幾點上床睡覺？

Iris didn't get out of bed till lunchtime today.

Iris今天直到午餐時間才下床。

Peter likes to have breakfast in bed on a Saturday morning.

Peter星期天時喜歡在床上吃早餐。

Why can't you kids make your own beds?

你們這些孩子怎麼不會自己整理床鋪？

mattress (n.) 床墊

詞彙：

a firm/soft mattress 一個硬的／軟的床墊

pillow (n.) 枕頭

詞彙：

pillowcase 枕頭套

pillow fight 枕頭戰

例句：

I'll be asleep as soon as my head hits the pillow.

當我的頭碰到枕頭時我將立刻入睡！

Do you prefer a feather pillow or foam pillow?

你喜歡羽絨枕還是泡綿枕？

sheet (n.) 床單

例句：

Tony put clean sheets on the bed.

Tony鋪上乾淨的床單。

I've changed the sheet this morning.

我今天早上已經換過床單。

MP3 146

alarm clock (n.) 鬧鐘

片語：

set the alarm clock 設定鬧鐘

例句：

Have you set the alarm clock?

Yes, I've set the alarm for 7.30.

你設定好鬧鐘時間了嗎？

有的！我定七點半！

Turn off the alarm clock!

把鬧鐘關掉！

Didn't you hear your alarm clock going off this morning?

你早上難道沒有聽到你的鬧鐘響？

My alarm clock went off at 6:00.

我的鬧鐘六點響。

headboard (n.) 床頭版

nightstand/night table (n.)

床邊桌、床邊櫃

comforter/quilt (n.) 棉被

(英式英語：duvet)

vanity/dressing table (n.) 梳妝台

makeup (n.) 化妝

例句：

She always wears a lot of makeup.

她總是畫濃妝。

Judy's hair looked untidy, and she had no makeup on.

Judy披頭散髮，臉上也沒有上妝。

Jennifer was still putting on her makeup when the taxi arrived.

當計程車抵達時，Jennifer仍在化妝。

MP3 147

perfume (n.) 香水

詞彙：

a bottle of perfume 一瓶香水

例句：

What perfume are you wearing?

你搽什麼香水？

She was wearing the perfume that he'd bought her.

她搽上他之前送的香水。

cologne (n.) 古龍水

deodorant (n.) 止汗劑

lipstick (n.) 口紅

blush (n.) 腮紅

nail polish (n.) 指甲油

nail polish remover (n.) 去光水

foundation (n.) 粉底

eyeliner (n.) 眼線筆

eye shadow (n.) 眼影

mascara (n.) 睫毛膏

MP3 148

起居：

living room (n.) 客廳

例句：

There is a large living room which has a sliding door leading onto the garden.

有一個寬敞的客廳，透過滑門可以通往花園。

lamp (n.) 燈

詞彙：

street lamp 街燈

floor lamp 立燈

table lamp 桌燈

desk lamp 檯燈

bedside lamp 床頭燈

例句：

Father enjoys reading newspaper by the floor lamp.

爸爸最喜歡在立燈邊讀報。

sofa (n.) 沙發

例句：

This large four-seater sofa can be converted into a double bed.

這個碩大的四人座沙發可以變成一個雙人床。

armchair (n.) 單人沙發、扶手椅

例句：

My grandfather loves to sit in his armchair by the fire and read the newspaper.

我的祖父最愛坐在火爐邊的扶手椅上讀報。

cushion (n.) 抱枕、靠墊、坐墊

詞彙：

MP3 149

scatter cushion 靠墊、抱枕

例句：

David sank back against/into the cushions.

David整個陷進靠墊裡。

A few scatter cushions would help brighten up that old sofa.

幾個抱枕就能讓那張老舊的沙發變得亮眼。

carpet (n.) 地毯

例句：

We've just had a new carpet laid in our bedroom.

我們的臥室剛剛鋪上新地毯。

rug (n.) 小一點的地毯

例句：

The dog lies on the rug in front of the fireplace.

那隻狗躺在壁爐前的地毯上。

window (n.) 窗戶

片語：

open/close a window

例句：

Is it alright if I open the window?

我可以打開這扇窗嗎？

The teacher caught me staring out of the window.

老師逮到我凝視窗外。

drapes (n.) 窗簾（英式英語：curtains）

例句：

We pulled the drapes and switched the light on.

我們拉上窗簾並且開燈。

Shall I open the curtains?

我可以打開窗簾嗎？

clock (n.) 鐘

例句：

I think the clock is fast/slow.

我覺得這個鐘快了／慢了。

I lay there listening to the clock ticking.

我躺在那兒聽著時鐘滴答滴答走。

The clock stopped.

這時鐘停了。

bookshelf (n.) 書架

例句：

This book is a must for every child's bookshelf.

這是一本每個孩子書架上必備的書。

telephone (n.) 電話

片語：

pick up/answer the telephone 接電話

use the phone 打電話

例句：

They've got a telephone in the living room.

他們有一具電話在客廳。

I was on the telephone when he came in.

當他進來時我正在電話中。

Can I use the telephone?

我可以打電話嗎？

Reservations can be made by telephone.

可以用電話預約。

television (n.) 電視

詞彙：

a 3D/HD/widescreen television

一個3D／高畫質／寬螢幕的電視

television producer/reporter/presenter

電視製作人／記者／主持人

MP3 151

digital/cable television 數位／有線電視

public television 公共電視

TV stand 電視櫃、電視架

片語：

turn/switch a television on/off 開／關電視

turn the television up/down 將電視音量調高／低

例句：

They just sit in front of the television all day.

他們在電視機前坐了一天。

Your problem is that you watch too much television.

你的問題就是看太多電視。

Is there anything interesting on television tonight?

今晚有什麼有趣的電視節目？

fireplace (n.) 壁爐

例句：

Kelly swept the ashes from the fireplace.

Kelly清理壁爐裡的灰燼。

chimney (n.) 煙囪

例句：

Sweep the chimney at least once a year.

一年至少清理一次煙囪。

vase (n.) 花瓶

詞彙：

a vase of roses 一花瓶玫瑰

例句：

Teresa put the fresh flowers in a vase.

Teresa將鮮花插在花瓶裡。

wallpaper (n.) 壁紙

詞彙：

a roll of wallpaper 一卷壁紙

例句：

We thought we'd put up some wallpaper in the children's bedroom to make it brighter.

我們考慮在孩子們的房間貼上壁紙讓它變得更明亮。

coffee table (n.) 茶几

side table (n.) 邊桌

vacuum cleaner (n.) 吸塵器

(英式英語：Hoover)

動詞：

vacuum/hoover 吸地

brush/broom (n.) 掃把

(brush有時也有刷子的意思)

詞彙：

a witch's broom 女巫的掃帚

例句：

Please remove any loose dirt with the brush.

用掃把掃掉散落的灰塵。

mop (n./v.) 拖把、拖地

例句：

Don't go in the living room. My mother just finished mopping the floor.

現在別進客廳，我媽才剛擦完地板。

bucket (n.) 水桶

詞彙：

a bucket of water 一桶水

例句：

Armed with a bucket and a mop, Joseph started washing the floor.

準備好水桶和拖把(mop)，Joseph開始清洗地板。

MP3 153

sweep (v.) 打掃、清掃

片語：

sweep the floor 掃地

例句：

Will you sweep up the patio?

你要打掃露臺嗎？

wipe (v.) 擦乾、抹、揩、擦拭

例句：

The waiter wiped the table before we sat down.

服務生在我們入座前擦了桌子。

Nadia wiped away her tears.

Nadia揩掉她的淚。

rub (v./n.) 摩擦、搓、揉、擦洗

片語：

rub your nose/chin/eyes/forehead

揉鼻子／摩下巴／揉眼睛／摩額頭

例句：

She rubbed her eyes sleepily.

她睡眼惺忪地揉揉眼睛。

Iris rubs her hair with a towel.

Iris用毛巾擦頭髮。

rinse (v.) 沖洗、漱口

例句：

Rinse the vegetables under a cold tap for two minutes.

將蔬菜放在冷水龍頭下沖洗兩分鐘。

Rinse your mouth with mouthwash.

用漱口水漱口。

國家圖書館出版品預行編目資料

英文單字只要會這些就夠 / 許純華著.
-- 初版. -- 新北市 : 雅典文化, 民104.04
面 ; 公分. -- (全民學英文 ; 38)
ISBN 978-986-5753-38-2(平裝附光碟片)
1.英語 2.詞彙
805.12 104002328

全民學英文系列 38

英文單字只要會這些就夠

作者／許純華
責編／許純華
美術編輯／林家維
封面設計／劉逸芹

法律顧問：方圓法律事務所／涂成樞律師

總經銷：永續圖書有限公司
永續圖書線上購物網
www.foreverbooks.com.tw

CVS代理／美璟文化有限公司
TEL：（02）2723-9968
FAX：（02）2723-9668

出版日／2015年4月

雅典文化

出版社
22103 新北市汐止區大同路三段194號9樓之1
TEL （02）8647-3663
FAX （02）8647-3660

版權所有，任何形式之翻印，均屬侵權行為

全民學英文
38

英文單字只要會這些就夠

雅致風靡　典藏文化

親愛的顧客您好，感謝您購買這本書。即日起，填寫讀者回函卡寄回至本公司，我們每月將抽出一百名回函讀者，寄出精美禮物並享有生日當月購書優惠！想知道更多更即時的消息，歡迎加入"永續圖書粉絲團"

您也可以選擇傳真、掃描或用本公司準備的免郵回函寄回，謝謝。

傳真電話：（02）8647-3660　　電子信箱：yungjiuh@ms45.hinet.net

姓名：　　　　性別：　□男　□女

出生日期：　年　月　日　電話：

學歷：　　　　職業：

E-mail：

地址：□□□

從何處購買此書：　　　　購買金額：　　元

購買本書動機：□封面 □書名 □排版 □內容 □作者 □偶然衝動

你對本書的意見：
內容：□滿意□尚可□待改進　編輯：□滿意□尚可□待改進
封面：□滿意□尚可□待改進　定價：□滿意□尚可□待改進

其他建議：

總經銷：永續圖書有限公司

永續圖書線上購物網

www.foreverbooks.com.tw

您可以使用以下方式將回函寄回。

您的回覆，是我們進步的最大動力，謝謝。

① 使用本公司準備的免郵回函寄回。

② 傳真電話：（02）8647-3660

③ 掃描圖檔寄到電子信箱：

yungjiuh@ms45.hinet.net

沿此線對折後寄回，謝謝。

廣 告 回 信
基隆郵局登記證
基隆廣字第056號

221-03

雅典文化事業有限公司　收

新北市汐止區大同路三段194號9樓之1

雅致風靡　典藏文化

YADAN